THE DEAD
SHOW

THE LIFE AFTER SERIES

THE DEAD SHOW

AMANDA FASCIANO

4 Horsemen
Publications, Inc.

This Book is Dedicated To

Anthony, Finley, and Joseph Fasciano. Without all of you putting up with my craziness, none of this would be possible. Thank you for letting me follow my dreams.

Dr. Eric O'Dierno, my very own personal Dr. Venkman, for his patience in putting up with my questions regarding scientific information.

Table of Contents

CHAPTER 1

The Nightmare

*S*now felt white-hot rage shoot through him as he saw Cadence Riley, his partner and someone he cared about, caged above a fire like she was some animal being roasted. He saw the state of her legs, or what remained of them, and then the robed form of the man who was responsible. Osmund Snow, a spirit who was always calm and sensible, felt only incomprehensible anger as he quickly closed the distance between Marcus Overton and himself. Snow was intent on causing as much harm to the other ghost as he could. He saw Sam Riley out of the corner of his eye and knew that even though the young man was wounded, he would do everything he could to get his sister out of the cage.

The powerful blow that Snow dealt to Overton's face filled him with satisfaction, seeing the silvery blood explode from the man's nose. He wrestled for the knife, which the robed man had stolen from Cadence when he had overpowered her. He managed to finally get it away from Overton, and Snow sank the blade of it deep into the man's leg. There was no way he was letting Overton get out of here after all of the evil he had done.

A scream of pain erupted from Cadence as Sam worked at freeing her, not only from the ties that bound her to the chair inside the cage, but by separating what was left of her charred limbs from the chair. Snow scowled and grabbed a handful of Overton's robes, dragging the man, kicking and screaming no less, toward the cage. He knew that the area they were in was a so-called null. No ghostly powers or magic could be used here. Snow knew a way around that, however.

He reached the door of the cage, dragging Overton behind him. He pointed at the lock and a bright silver-white light arced between his finger and the mechanism, releasing it. Sam, who had been wounded himself after triggering a booby trap as they had come in, scrambled to get his sister out of the cage. Cadence was on the verge of passing out, both from the pain she was in and the damage that had been done to her. Snow felt that spike of rage, somehow both burning and freezing him at the same time, and shoved Overton into the cage. For his part, Overton begged and pleaded, promising them anything to set him free. Sam was already moving away from the cage, carrying the unconscious form of his sister. Snow turned a deaf ear to Overton's pleas and, using the same power as before, light arced between his finger and the lock once more. Snow put even more energy into it, making sure that the latch fused shut.

Sam began to hurry away as best as he could, carrying his unconscious sister over his unwounded shoulder. Snow followed but paused by the lever that operated the sliding trapdoor. He knew that door hid the flames that had half-roasted his partner. All he had to do was flip that lever and not only would the beaten and bloody Overton be trapped in that cage forever, but he would burn forever, too. Snow heard Sam call out to him to hurry. He turned to follow the young man but then spun on his heel and threw the lever, throwing open the trapdoor and letting the flames rise up. Overton howled in pain.

Snow turned once more to leave, but a mirror he didn't remember seeing in here before caught his eye. In it, he found his reflection to be that of Overton. Fear shot through him just as the rage had before. He turned to the cage and saw himself in it, the flames of the fire beneath licking around the metallic cage and curling around the floor to caress his feet and legs.

"No!" he shouted, sitting upright in his office chair, the force of the movement rolling him back from his desk a bit. His breathing was heavy, and he could feel the sweat on his forehead.

"Nightmares?" a deep, smooth male voice asked from where Cadence's desk was. Snow looked over to see the dark-skinned form of his former mentor, Alistair Croft. He gave the man a sheepish smile.

"Silly, isn't it?" Snow asked in his usual clipped British accent. "Whoever heard of a ghost having nightmares? After all, what do we have to be afraid of? We're dead."

"Just because we're dead doesn't mean we don't have fears. Especially for those of us who continue to fight to protect others. I have found, through personal experience, believe me, that we fear becoming the monsters we fight," Alistair said with a shrug before leaning forward. "You've been very good at avoiding me, Osmund. But we need to talk. I know you used the manipulation of power I taught you."

Snow pressed his lips together as he considered his response. Alistair was right, of course. He had been avoiding him because he had wanted to prevent this very conversation. Snow anticipated that this was going to be about as unpleasant as the nightmare he had just awoken from. Finally, he settled on the simple truth, waiting to see where Alistair took it from there. "I did."

"Why?" Croft asked. There was no admonishment or judgment in his tone, just pure curiosity.

"It was the most expedient way of getting her out of that cage. You and Whitfield had given us something of a time limit with that ritual to seal the vessel."

Croft nodded at length and steepled his fingers as he folded his hands in front of him. "You risked a lot to save her. I know you care for her, but to use that trick in a place like that? Osmund, that was dangerous."

"Would you rather I have taken the time to root through Overton's clothes for a key to the cage? And if it hadn't been on him, what then? Search the room? Each second that went by was a second closer to all of us getting trapped in that vessel, and you know it. We barely got out in time as it was." Snow was aware of how defensive he sounded, and he didn't like it, but he spoke the truth. The portal had closed, and the vessel had sealed mere seconds after they stepped out of it.

Alistair seemed to think about this and nodded slowly. "You're fortunate he either didn't know how to, or couldn't, counter it. Then you would have spent part of your soul for nothing."

"I knew the risks," Snow said, his voice quiet. While he did know the risks, he couldn't, in all honesty, say that he had been aware of them at the time. He had acted without thinking, which was a rarity for him.

"Are the nightmares simply left over from that experience, or is something else bothering you?"

Snow rose with a sigh and began to pace back and forth behind his desk. "Sam told you, in quite exciting detail, about what happened while we were in there."

"Yes, he did." Alistair chuckled. "I think it was a mix of the exuberance of youth and getting to finally do something other than babysit the other murder victims' spirits."

"There was one thing he didn't tell you, one thing he didn't know." Snow paused once more, pressing his lips together. He wanted to confess his struggle with pulling the lever or not, but he also found that he was afraid that speaking it aloud would make it more reprehensible. That confessing to that much of a desire to do harm would make him evil, or as Alistair had said, "a monster."

Croft rose from the seat at Cadence's desk and moved over to Snow, putting a hand on his old friend's shoulder. "Osmund, talk to me. What is it that bothers you so much?"

"The cage he had Cadence in was over a trapdoor. A lever pulled the trapdoor open and let the flames come up to burn the person in the cage."

"Right, I knew about that," Alistair agreed. He could see where Snow was heading, but also knew the man needed to say it out loud to get it out of his system.

"Once I had him locked in the cage, and we were leaving..." Snow trailed off and sat down with a heavy sigh, cradling his head in his hands. "God, Alistair, I wanted to pull that lever so badly. I wanted him to burn. I wanted him to suffer in pain for all of the pain he caused over the years. I was so angry at what he did to Cadence..." Again, he trailed off as his shoulders shook. "I wanted to hear him scream as he had made Cadence scream."

"You have to say it." Alistair tried to prompt his former protégé into admitting what his real motivation had been.

Snow let his hands fall to the desk and balled them into fists, his shoulders now still and his voice flat and cold when he spoke. "I wanted revenge."

"Good," Alistair said.

"Good?" Snow questioned. Shock and disbelief were evident on his face as he turned to face his former mentor.

"Yes. Good that you finally said what you were feeling, what you were struggling with." Alistair sat back down in Cadence's chair. "Or did you forget that, like your special ability with machinery and electronics, I have special sight? I could see it running through you like poison running through your veins. It was keeping you from healing the parts of your soul you spent. I thought you might work through it on your own, so I let you be. But to find you asleep at your desk? The nightmare you were having? That showed me I had to push you."

"Push me to what? Admit I'm a monster?" Snow's tone was bitter.

"Push you to admit that you wanted revenge and that you are afraid that wanting revenge makes you a monster."

"Alistair, you said yourself that the only thing that separates us from beings like that are our actions."

"Exactly." Croft leaned forward, toward Snow. "You didn't act on the impulse to pull the lever. Every one of us, alive or dead, can have dark thoughts. Don't persecute yourself for such a human thing. You didn't act on the impulse. That, my friend, is what's important. The fact that you are wracking yourself with guilt over it only verifies the fact that you are not what you fear. A monster wouldn't care."

Snow nodded slowly, hearing Croft's words. While a small part of him still wanted to argue, he realized Croft was right. Even though he had been tempted, very tempted, to pull that lever, he had not. The thought didn't make him evil.

"I do need to ask a delicate question of you, however," Croft continued.

"Oh?"

"I'm not going to deny that your anger and the power you used helped save your partner and get the three of you out of an awful situation. You said the anger came from seeing what he had done to Cadence, that you wanted revenge for her. What exactly are your feelings for Detective Riley?"

Snow sat back in his chair, not quite believing Croft was asking him that question. "Alistair, you cannot be suggesting "

Croft cut him off. "I am suggesting nothing. I am merely asking where you and your partner stand with each other."

"I trust her with my life, such as it is, and I know she trusts me with hers. We're friends. There is nothing romantic between us."

"I know that, Osmund. I wasn't suggesting romantic. I believe our good Doctor Suarez has that covered, as much as our detective might publicly bristle at the notion. No, Osmund. What I have heard and what you have admitted … it sounds more like a father protecting his daughter."

"The days of me missing my children are long gone, old friend. They are grown, had families of their own, and some may have even passed on already. I am not trying to replace what I had when I was alive. I am protective of her; I think in any kind of partnership you have that, especially one that requires the trust and comradery that ours does."

Croft nodded a bit. "I simply had to make sure."

"Your sight didn't let you see that?" Snow asked, half teasing his old mentor and partner.

"No," Croft responded with a smile as he rose from his seat at Cadence's desk. "I could only see that your soul was not mending and that something was poisoning you. I hope now you can begin to heal. Now go home and get some sleep. That's an order."

"Yes, sir." Snow rose to follow Croft out of the office he shared with Cadence and their other partner, Whitfield.

CHAPTER 2

Waking Up

The first thing Cadence was aware of was that someone was holding her hand. She opened her eyes and recognized the hospital room as the same one she had woken in before. This time, there were far fewer people in the room. There was also a lot less pain in her legs than there had been the last time she woke. She saw Ramon on her left, his short brown hair as unmistakable to her as her brother's tousled bright blonde locks. Ramon had pulled a chair up beside her bed and had fallen asleep holding her hand. *How long had she been asleep this time?*

Cadence gave Ramon's hand a gentle squeeze. "What's up, doc?" she said with a bit of a smile.

Ramon shifted in the chair as he opened his eyes. It took a moment for him to register that Cadence was awake, and he sat forward as he realized it. "Hey, sleepyhead," he greeted, looking far more relieved than Cadence was comfortable with.

"Sleepyhead, huh?" she asked, narrowing her eyes. "How long have I been sleeping this time?" Last time, they had let her sleep for a week before she woke up. Prior to that, it had been three days, right after they had gotten her out of Overton's prison.

"About a month." Ramon quickly kept talking as he saw her eyes widen and her mouth open to reply. "Before you get angry, you need to know that the damage was extensive, and you needed that rest to heal."

Cadence closed her mouth on her initial reply as her anger at being left to sleep for so long faded. She knew he was right. She remembered how much pain she had felt when she had awoken the first time in this room. Ramon watched the anger fade from her eyes and face and let go of a breath he hadn't realized he was holding. He smiled and rose from his chair, stretching.

"So, it's been about five weeks, then? Because last time you said it had been a week that I had been asleep, right? Or was the month including that?"

"Five weeks," Ramon said. "It's been five weeks since they got you out of that hellhole." There was an underlying anger in his voice that made Cadence lift an eyebrow in surprise.

"I don't think I've ever heard that tone from you before," she commented.

"I'm allowed to be angry about what was done to you. Even if there were no personal feelings involved, I would still be angry about what Overton did to you. No one should have to go through such pain." The caveat of "if there were no personal feelings involved" made Cadence smile a little.

"Well, there seems to be less pain now than there was before." Cade hoped to turn him from that topic. "And I'm awake, so progress, right?"

"Yes," he said with a smile to her. "Let's take a look. I should warn you, though, there are scars. There will likely always be scars from that." Again, she could hear the anger beneath his voice.

"Scars I can live with. No more open wounds, though, right?" she asked with a hopeful look.

Ramon laughed and shook his head. "No, nothing is open anymore."

"What's so funny?" Her tone of voice was indignant as she asked the question. She knew what he was laughing at. He had teased her for it before. She just wanted to distract him from his anger.

"It's funny to me." He gave a shrug of his shoulders as he grabbed the sheet. "The idea of a hardened detective so afraid of the sight of blood."

"Oh, I can take the sight of blood, no problem. Just not my own." Cade added the last with a sheepish look and a bit of a shrug. She had told him that before, after the chaos creature had attacked her and nearly eaten her at Lexington Hills. But familiar conversation was a good way to distract both of them from the anger and pain.

Ramon chuckled and pulled the sheet covering her legs down. Cadence saw that he hadn't been joking. There was a multitude of scars. Silvery scars covered most of her legs. It looked like spider webs on her thighs and knees, the threads of which got thicker and closer together as they went lower on her legs. Her ankles and feet were so covered they looked like they had been painted entirely silver. Ramon observed her face as she took in the damage.

"Well," she said at length, "looks like I can get a second job using my feet as disco balls."

Ramon smiled, though he knew her well enough by now to know that humor was her defense mechanism. "Try moving your feet a little; tell me if there is any pain."

Cadence dutifully wiggled her toes and turned her feet in circles from the ankles. She was stiff and sore, wincing a little as she did, but it wasn't the searing pain it had been a month ago. Ramon kept careful watch, noting where she winced and noticing the somewhat limited movement of her feet and ankles. To Cade, the scarring on her feet felt like leather straps that were wound too tight against her, restricting her movements.

"Now comes the hard part." He offered her his hand. "Let's see if you can stand."

"And if I can't?" Cadence looked up at him, afraid of what his answer might be.

"We'll cross that bridge if we come to it." He nodded to her in encouragement. "You can do this. Aside from Ruby, I've not met a more stubborn, determined woman."

"You're one of the few men I've met who can say that and not make it sound like a bad thing," she said, taking his hand. She felt the butterflies in her stomach as she moved, still apprehensive about what would happen if there was a problem with being able to walk. She liked where she was, what she was doing, and the people around her. She didn't want it to change. She winced a little as her feet touched the floor, but the face she made was more the anticipation of the pain, rather than any pain she felt. Her movements were slow and careful as she eased herself off the bed and onto her feet. It hurt; there was no denying that, but not nearly as bad as it had before.

"Okay, good." Ramon kept hold of her hand for support as he watched her movements. "How do you feel?"

"I'm okay, I think," she said as she tested out her feet. "It hurts a little still, and it feels weird. But considering where I was a month ago, this is definitely an improvement."

"What do you mean when you say it feels weird?"

"It's like..." She paused for a moment, trying to think of the best way to phrase it. "It's kind of like my feet and ankles have been wrapped up in a thick leather bandage."

"That makes sense, given the condition they are in," Ramon said. "But you are right; that is much better than before. I think things will get easier as you move around more."

"Does that mean I can get out of here?" Cade asked with a hopeful smile.

"Ready to leave me so fast?" he teased.

"You? Hell no. A hospital room? Hell yes," she answered, taking a tentative step forward. Ramon still had hold of her hand, and he let her use him as support as she tested out walking. She didn't lean on him much, which he was relieved to see. They walked around the room together at a slow, steady pace, circling back to the bed.

"Okay, let me see your feet after that. Back in bed," Ramon directed.

"How long have you been waiting to say that to me?" she joked. He made a face halfway between amusement and annoyance. She grinned in return and got back into the bed as Ramon knelt to examine her feet.

"Excellent, nothing reopened," Ramon said. He rose from his knees and smiled at her. "I think this means you are clear to go and return to duty. That should make both you and Snow happy."

"Well, I know it makes me happy," Cade said with a smile. "How is everyone? Have you seen them at all?"

"Snow and your brother Sam, I see here almost daily. Mr. Croft has come in a few times as well. They seem to be doing well, but I know they have all been worried about you," Ramon said. "As have I." He leaned in and kissed her gently on the cheek.

"So, with this new gig you have here, being a doctor, are you stuck here all the time like you were at Lexington, or do you get time off?" Cade asked.

Ramon smiled. "I get time off. Though I've not left the hospital yet."

Cadence understood what he meant without him having to explain. When she awoke, he had been sleeping in the chair, holding her hand. He had been spending his free time in here, with her. "Well, now you'll have to," she said. "I won't be so convenient to visit anymore."

"With your track record?" Ramon laughed. "You'll be back here within two weeks."

"Hey, I can take care of myself very well, thank you. At least I could when I was alive," Cade added with a sigh. She hated the fact that she kept getting hurt in this new life. It chafed her to no end that Sam and Snow had to rescue her. She had never liked damsels in distress, and now she had been one.

"Hey, you're okay," Ramon comforted as he lifted his hand to caress her cheek. He had known that this entire situation was not going to sit well with her. Her strength and stubbornness made it difficult to accept any situation in which she might need help. "You're not even a year dead yet, and you've gone up against some very tough obstacles. Obstacles that had killed other people, both dead and alive. I think you've been doing better than anyone could reasonably expect of any spirit."

"But you're not biased at all," she said with a bit of a smirk.

He smiled back at her, tenderness in his brown eyes. "Not at all."

CHAPTER 3

Returning to Duty

Snow had gone back to his home as Croft had ordered, and his sleep had been dream free, which he was thankful for. He felt more rested than he had in several weeks, ready to tackle the cases he knew they had pending. His thoughts about what he had to do for the day ceased as he stopped short in the doorway to his office. There, seated at his desk, with her feet propped up on it, was his partner.

"It's been so long, I forget. This is my desk, right?" Cade asked the question with a knowing grin. She knew it was his desk; she was doing it to get a rise out of him.

To her mild disappointment, he didn't even pretend to look irked. He seemed shocked at first, and then a large smile spread across his face. He finished entering the office and closed the door behind him. Cadence watched him as he crossed the room, keeping his silence but continuing to smile. He took a seat at her desk and folded his hands in front of him.

"Oh, come on," she said. "I haven't been able to be a pain in your ass for five weeks. When I finally can, you're just going to take it?"

"I am so happy to see you up and about; I couldn't care less which desk you sit at," he said.

"Damn, you're going soft on me, Ozzie," she said. She knew the nickname would irk him; it always did.

To her gratification, Snow rolled his eyes as he heard her call him that irritating name. "Why didn't you let me know you were released?" Snow made a mental note to chastise Ramon for not letting him know, either. "When I stopped by yesterday, you were still out cold. Ramon said you hadn't woken up yet."

"I woke up last night. It was late," Cadence said with a slight shrug. "When Ramon brought me home, Sam was fast asleep on my couch. I figured I would wait to let you guys know until this morning. Of course, I got up, and Sam was gone, but he left a note for me, so he must have figured it out. The closed bedroom door might have been a clue. I thought he would be here or be with you. Where is he?"

"Ah, yes, there is quite a bit of catching up to do, isn't there?" he said.

"Is there? What have I missed?"

"Well, as you asked about your brother, I will answer that first. Sam has found a new calling." Snow put up his hands to indicate that Cadence needed to let him finish.

He could tell from her look of concern that she had not been expecting this. "He is a guardian now."

"A guardian? Of what, the galaxy?" she asked, referencing her brother's favorite comic book when they had been young.

Snow was confused for a moment, then shook his head, realizing that she was confusing what he meant for something else. "No, he is like a guardian angel; I think that would be the closest thing to it. Sometimes spirits have connections with mediums and psychics and can become their guardians or guides. They protect the psychic from other spirits that would try to harm or overpower the psychic."

"So, he is playing protector for a breather after spending ten years playing babysitter for dead co-eds," Cadence said. "That hardly seems fair. How did this get determined, anyway?"

"It was discovered that he has a strong natural connection with someone," Snow said, skirting around the topic.

"When I woke up a month ago, I think he was still following you around, right?"

"Yes," Snow said with a nod.

"Well, in our time together, we've only regularly encountered one psychic. Wait, so you're telling me he's Lauren's spirit guide or guardian?" Cadence took her feet off Snow's desk and sat up. She winced just a bit when her feet hit the floor, and the flinch was not missed by Snow.

"Yes, that is exactly what I am telling you. Are you certain you're alright to be here? You appear to still be in pain."

"Yep, Ramon cleared me to come back." Cadence waved away Snow's concern. "I'll probably be dealing with a little bit of pain for a while more, but it is nothing near as bad as it was. Ramon said he would let Croft know this morning that I was good to go. Now I seem to remember you saying that Lauren's group had been contacted by a television show. What came of that?"

"That is quickly approaching and one reason I am concerned about your still being in pain. Do you think you will be up to the task of policing an investigation in an old prison? Those areas are not known for having well-behaved ghosts." Snow moved and perched on the corner of his desk as they spoke.

"I'm fine." Cadence nodded. "As I said, am I sore. Sure. It's going to take a little time not to be, according to Ramon. But I am more than ready to go. Besides, you know Ramon, there is absolutely no way he would have cleared me to come back to work if he wasn't certain it was safe for me. No matter how much of a pain in the ass patient I am."

"You are right about that. The good doctor wouldn't put you in harm's way if you weren't up to the task of defending yourself." Snow frowned a bit, his own concern for his partner showing. But he knew she was right in that Ramon would never have released her for work if he hadn't thought she had healed enough to be up to it.

"So, you said the television show thing is quickly approaching. How soon?" Cadence asked as she carefully rose from Snow's chair and made her way around to her own desk. Her movements were slow and deliberate, and she had a limp, but she made it.

"We'll find out today, actually. Our group of investigators is having a meeting at the shop this morning where they expect a phone call from the producer to give them the final information and to confirm dates," Snow said.

"And Sam will already be there because he is Lauren's guardian now, correct?" Cadence was more or less reiterating things to make sure she had what she needed to know locked down in her mind.

"Yes," Snow said with a nod.

"What about Whitfield? Where is he?" Cade asked.

"He should be at the meeting this morning. NHD work has been keeping him quite busy of late," Snow said.

"Anything we should know about? I mean, we are still Croft's pet project, right? The breakdown was supposed to be that he is with us unless we don't need him, then he reports to the NHD, on loan from us, right?"

Snow lifted an eyebrow as his mouth crooked in amusement. "One of these days, I will be the one rubbing off on you, and you will finally use proper English. Yes, our unit is the same, with the same mission and the same personnel. But the situation with Whitfield seems to be fluid. Apparently, there has been a severe shortage in the Non-Human Division. Agents have been going missing or winding up victims of the non-humans they are trying to deal with. The NHD asked to borrow him back from us, since our team was taking it slowly without you."

"There are non-humans at the prison?" Cadence asked in surprise.

"It wouldn't be out of the question, given all of the negative energy and deaths that took place there," Snow said.

"Good point." Cadence nodded.

"There is one more thing you should be aware of before we get too far caught up in our normal day-to-day emergencies." Snow took a moment to gather his thoughts. He'd had a month to figure out how to explain this to her, but it still seemed just too crazy to be real.

Cadence frowned as she saw Snow hesitating. "Spit it out, Ozzie."

"The whole thing with Overton and the demon that he was trying to summon is apparently part of a larger scheme."

"What kind of larger scheme?" Cade leaned forward a little as she asked the question. The concept sounded familiar to her, the word "global" ringing in her head for some reason. But she couldn't quite remember.

"According to Alistair, there has been a plot afoot for a while to have spirits retake the earth in a way. To possess willing breathers and use non-human creatures in servitude to our kind to force other breathers to comply."

Cadence blinked as she processed this, then shook her head. "That's crazy."

"That's what we said, too, when he informed us of it," Snow said.

"When did he tell you all about this?"

"As we were putting together the plan to save you from Overton's prison. We'd not yet had the chance to really brief you on what we learned," Snow said.

Cadence blinked again, her eyebrows lifting high as she tried to rationalize what she had just been told. "Okay, so this bad guy, or guys, wants to free non-humans and somehow leash them like they were dogs. These guys want our kind to possess people, and any breather who tries to fight back or refuses, they turn their pet non-human on until the breather cooperates. Is that about the gist of it?"

Snow nodded solemnly. "It sounds like you have a good grasp of it, yes."

"It's insane," she reiterated. "How long has this plot been going on? How long has Croft known about it?"

"Longer than you've been dead," Croft said, his deep melodious voice coming from the office doorway behind Cadence.

"That doesn't take much; I've been dead less than a year," Cadence said, her tone dry. "And how is it you always manage to show up at the right time?" she added, half turning in her chair to face him.

Croft smiled, spreading his hands as he shrugged; his white teeth were a sharp contrast to his dark brown skin. "Why do you think I'm the boss?"

"That wasn't an answer," Cadence said, her tone hinting at grumpiness at the lack of response.

"Our good Doctor Suarez came to see me," Croft said, choosing to ignore Cadence's mood. "I was relieved to hear him say you were not only awake but clear to come back to work. We have great need of your talents, Detective Riley."

"Thank you, sir," Cade said, her voice and tone quiet as her mind was still chewing on what Snow had told her.

Croft moved into the room with the grace of a cat and stopped in between the two desks to speak to both of them.

"As far as I am aware, this plot has been going on for several decades now. Whoever is leading this plan has been patient, they have been quiet, and they have been slow, so we only found out about it a couple of years ago. That is one reason why you two hold the position that you do now. What the two of you have managed to accomplish in less than a year is astounding. You manage to keep thwarting this group's plans."

"Are you saying the chaos thing at Lexington Hills was because of these people?" It was Cadence who voiced the question.

"Given that this so-called Wolf was involved in both cases, and we know he was working with Overton, who was a ranking member of this cause of theirs, yes," Croft said.

"So, should we just start tailing Wolf?" Cadence asked.

"Do you know how to find him?" Croft countered.

"Oh," Cade said, deflating a little as she leaned back in her chair. "No."

"So, for now, keep going as you are. I'm sure this television case will prove difficult enough, and I don't know that you are up to squaring off against Wolf or any of his superiors just yet," Croft said. He reached out and put a hand on Cade's shoulder. "I am glad you are well and that you are back with us, Cadence."

"Thank you, sir," she said with a smile. "I'm glad to be back."

CHAPTER 4

The Gang's Back Together

Lauren stood at the counter in her New Age shop, cordless phone pressed to her ear beneath her wavy black hair. The Rubenesque woman, who was getting closer to middle-aged every day, had a pad of paper on the glass-topped counter in front of her, the pen in her hand leaving hurried notes on the paper in blue ink. Aidan, who looked just as he had five weeks ago, with his shaggy brown hair and goatee, leaned against the counter, straining his ears to eavesdrop on what he could, watching the notes appear on the paper. Sam was unobtrusive and unobserved by the breathers as he stayed near Lauren, as well. All of them looked over when the chimes by the window made music, signifying the presence of spirits.

Snow walked past the chimes with Cadence limping along beside him. Sam had been aware that Cadence had been released from the hospital; he had peeked into her room and seen a sister-sized lump covered by blankets in her bed. What he hadn't known was that she had been cleared to return to work. Sam's face lit up as he saw her and he was beside her in an instant, giving her a huge hug.

"Hey, just because we're dead doesn't mean you get to squeeze the life out of me all over again." Her voice squeaked a bit from the force of his hug. Snow chuckled at the exuberance of the younger Riley sibling.

"I'm just happy to see you," Sam said, relief evident in his voice. "I was going to greet you when I got home. Are you good to be working, though? I see you limping." Worry creased his brow.

"Yeah, I'm okay. You think Ramon would let me out of his sight if I weren't? It's just going to take a little time for me to get all the way back to normal," Cadence said, tousling her brother's bright blond hair for good measure.

"Did Snow tell you what I'm doing now?" Sam asked, a bit of pride showing through in his emerald eyes.

"He did, and I'm proud of you," Cade said with a smile. She reached over to ruffle his hair again, and he ducked back, out of the way, to avoid it. "We're here for work, though, right now," she said as she pointed over to where Lauren still stood behind the glass counter on the phone. The three spirits made their way over to where Lauren and Aiden stood.

"Right, Barrington Prison," Lauren said with a nod, writing it down. "Wait, this weekend? I thought you guys weren't coming here for another couple of weeks."

There was silence as Lauren listened, and while the other three who were eavesdropping could hear a muffled male voice on the other end of the line, they couldn't make out the words. The person spoke for a while as Lauren listened and took notes on dates and times, noting a hotel name and number as well.

"No, that's fine. We'll be there." Lauren paused as she was asked a question. "Three: Myself, Aiden, and Derrick." There was another brief pause. "No, no, he passed away a few months ago. Yes, thank you."

Aiden winced as he heard her answer, knowing that could only be a question about Dan. Aiden went behind the counter and into the back room, getting the spirit box out. He knew that they had a bit to talk about with Snow. And Cadence, if she was back. As he made his way out of the back room and toward the table in the back of the store, the bells of the door rang out, and Derrick, the youngest of the ghost-hunting group, walked in.

"Yes, I have your number; we will call if we have any other questions," Lauren said as she nodded a greeting to Derrick. "We'll see you soon." She hung up the phone and looked at her piece of paper with its notes. With a sigh, she picked it up and took it over to the table, following Derrick to the back of the store.

Derrick noted the spirit box as Aiden set it down on the table. "They're here?"

"Think so," Aiden answered. "The chimes Lauren has set up went off. But before we talk to them, I want to find out what the guys on the phone were saying."

Lauren took a seat and placed the pad of paper neatly before her, the pen to one side. "Well, they've moved up the schedule. Apparently, some other place opened up to them, but only during the weekend they had initially set for us here. So, they moved us around on their schedule. They'll be here this weekend. If you had anything else going on, cancel it. We're going to be up to our eyeballs in work."

"I thought they just wanted us as guest advisors," Aiden said, folding his tall, lean body into a chair. "To interview us and then move on."

"That's changed, too," Lauren said with another sigh, irked at how chaotic this had become. "They'll be here Thursday night. They want us to meet with them at the restaurant in their hotel that night for dinner and to go over plans for the next day. Friday, they want to do exterior shots and our interviews. Then they want us at the prison with them on Saturday night, helping to investigate."

Aiden let out a whistle. "This is not going to be fun. That place has bad mojo."

"What do you mean?" Derrick asked.

"It just feels bad." Aiden shrugged. "Dan and I went there a couple of years ago. It is easy to get freaked out in that place. I'm not really sure how to describe it, other than evil."

"Well, it is a prison," Lauren said. "It's not like those who died there were angels."

"True," Aiden said as he reached over and turned the spirit box on. "Snow? You there?"

"I am," came the staticky version of Snow's clipped British voice from the round speaker.

"I'm assuming you heard that the TV show guys are going to be here this weekend, right?"

"Yes, I did, and I will add that your intuition about the place is correct. It houses some areas and spirits that can be very dangerous to the living."

"How dangerous?" Lauren asked.

"In my opinion, someone who wasn't being careful could easily find themselves on my side of the veil, leaving yours behind," Snow said, not putting too fine of a point on it.

"They could die?" Derrick asked in surprise, both his eyebrows and his voice lifting as he questioned this.

"It is possible," Snow said. "In some corners of that place, the less-than-savory characters have taken control. They could cause legitimate physical harm." The three living ghost hunters frowned at this and looked down at the table in response, thinking.

"Oh! Snow, is Cadence with you?" It was Derrick who asked.

"I'm here," Cadence said. "If only just."

"What do you mean?" It was Aiden posing the question this time.

"I was just given the clearance to return to work last night. This is my first day back," Cadence said.

Aiden let out a low whistle. "Damn. Five weeks out? That asshole must have really done a number on you."

"You have no idea, nor do you really want to," Cadence said, her voice gaining a sour note.

Snow cast a glance to the back office, where Lauren kept the urn that Overton was now imprisoned in. He hoped the man was still locked in the cage but was not about to try to go in to be sure. "Yes, but he is once again entrapped. With Detective Riley back in the field, things are returning to normal." Snow winced as he heard his voice coming out of the box. It went against all his ingrained rules to speak to breathers so plainly.

"I hope so," Lauren said. "I have a feeling we'll need all hands on deck for this." Snow was pleased to see that Lauren seemed to have finally moved on from blaming Cadence for Dan's death.

"If the TV guys have moved us up to this week," Derrick said, "what are we going to do about the Owens family? Do you think we can give both of these projects our full attention?"

"I think we can give the Owens family our undivided attention," Aiden said. "At least until Thursday night. We won't know more about what the TV show is going to want from us until then. Not to mention, maybe we will get lucky, and this family's issue is simply something along the lines of overexposure to EMF or bad plumbing."

"I sincerely doubt that, given what we know about it," Lauren said.

"What's going on with this Owens family?" Cadence's voice came through the speaker of the spirit box.

"The Owens family," Lauren said with a sigh as she turned pages in her notebook to reveal another page of notes. "The mother is convinced that the new invisible friend the young daughter has is a spirit. The father isn't convinced, but for the wife's peace of mind, he is willing to let us come in and investigate."

"How old is the Owens' little girl?" Cadence moved to look over Lauren's shoulder at the notepad.

"She's five years old," Lauren said in reply.

Snow asked the next question. "When do you plan on going to see this Owens family?" His voice coming out of the box was still jarring to him, but he was becoming used to it. As much as it rankled him to be breaking the rules so flagrantly, he had to admit it was expedient.

"They just got in touch with us yesterday," Derrick said. "I've been doing research on their property."

"We will head out to them tomorrow in the early afternoon. Mrs. Owens said the little girl has afternoon Pre-K, so we can do some initial talking and investigate without the child being there," Aiden said.

"We will be meeting here around noon if you want to ride along," Lauren offered.

"Thank you, I think we will," Snow said. "We'll do a little research on our end as well to see if we can't learn something. What's the address?"

Derrick gave them the address, and with the plans laid out for both investigations, Snow and Cadence exited the shop, the chimes in the window tinkling as they passed. In seconds, they were back in the large office that the two partners shared together with Whitfield and occasionally Bethany Saxon from the guidance department. The other two were not there, however, as Snow escorted Cadence to her desk before taking a seat at his own.

"Are you sure you're going to be up for this?" Snow had been quiet, but once they were finally settled in their office, he gave voice to the question that had been gnawing at him.

"Really? How many times do I have to answer this?" Cadence was a bit annoyed at Snow's question.

"Hear me out." Snow held up a hand to defer her answer. "I am well aware Dr. Suarez said you were clear to come back to work, but I'm not sure he knew you would be diving into such an investigation-heavy schedule, nor such a dangerous place as Barrington Prison."

Cadence nodded slowly. "I do see your point, and I appreciate your concern," she said at length, trying to measure her response properly, instead of just flying off the handle. She knew he wasn't saying she couldn't do the job, just that he was concerned it might be too taxing for her after having only just recovered. "I'll tell you what. I will let you know if I start feeling like it's too much, okay? And I promise not to ignore pain or tired-ness. But in promising you that, please, stop asking me if I am okay. I know you mean well, but it really grates on my nerves."

Snow canted his head to one side as he thought about what Cadence had said. "That sounds fair enough." He nodded. He gave her credit; she was growing. She hadn't just replied off the cuff with irritation or anger. She had thought about her response and had factored in why he was asking. "Then why don't you begin seeing if you can pull any information about the address of the Owens family while I see if I can track down Whitfield?" Snow suggested.

Cadence turned on her computer as they spoke. "Yeah, since I'm back, and it looks like we're going to need him," Cadence agreed.

"Which is why you are doing the research while I go retrieve him," Snow confirmed with a smile. Cadence nodded to Snow and gave him a salute, then turned back to her computer to see what she could dig up.

CHAPTER 5

Funny, It Doesn't Look Haunted

The chimes to the side of the door jangled delicately, indicating to the three ghost hunters gathered around one of the sales cases in the new age shop that at least one spirit had arrived. Lauren looked toward the chimes and smiled a little. Aiden and Derrick exchanged a quick look in reaction to Lauren's smile and shrugged.

"Snow and Cadence are here, let's go," Lauren said.

"Are they talking to you all the time now without needing the box?" It was Derrick who voiced the question, although both men were thinking it.

"Who else would it be?" Lauren said with a shake of her head. "Oh, come on. Process of elimination, guys. Catch up!" She walked around the case and made sure the sign on the door was flipped to "Closed." Derrick and

Aiden followed her out the door, and she took a moment to lock up before dropping her keys into her purse.

"It could always be a different spirit," Aiden said. "In this case, yeah, I'm sure you're right. But just because they come around a lot doesn't mean that it's always going to be them or even someone with good intentions."

Lauren smiled a little. She hadn't yet told the guys about Sam being around. She was afraid that his constant presence would weird them out a bit. She knew, however, that anything evil would have to go through him to get to her. That made her a bit more relaxed about the presence of spirits. She didn't know if it was a side effect of her being more relaxed, or if it was just a coincidence, but she had also noticed that her powers seemed to be growing. It could have been the familiarity she now had with Snow and Cadence, given how often they had come around, but she had been able to sense exactly which ghosts had come in and made the chimes go off.

Once they were settled in the van, with Aiden driving and Lauren riding shotgun, and Derrick, Snow, Sam, and Cade in the back, Lauren turned a little in her seat to look at Derrick. "Alright, research guru, what did you find out?"

"Well, as you know, I did research on the property," Derrick said. "Mrs. Owens was right in that it is new construction. The house was finished only a couple of months before they moved in. The property, on the other hand, used to be part of a larger parcel owned by the Barton family."

"As in THE Barton family?" Aiden looked back in the rearview mirror at Derrick in surprise. The Barton family was an old, wealthy, well-established family in the area. They were one of the founding families of the town.

Derrick nodded. "The very ones. The original Barton patriarch, James, gave the parcel of land to his son, Edgar, as a wedding gift. There was a tragedy several years later, and the entire house burned down, killing Edgar, his wife, and their two kids. Old-Man Barton had the remains of the estate on that land torn down and just let nature take it back. Three years ago, it was bought by the development company that built the neighborhood."

"But none of the other neighbors are reporting anything weird?" Aiden asked.

"If they're experiencing anything, they aren't telling anyone. None of my searches turned up anything," Derrick answered.

Lauren turned on the spirit box so that everyone could hear the spirits in the car reply as she asked, "What about on your end, guys? Did anything turn up?"

Cadence was the one to answer since, Snow hated hearing his own voice so much. "There hasn't been a reported haunting in that area at all, despite the tragedy that took place there. We did get a ping of energy about a mile away from the address about a month ago. We haven't had any reason before to have surveillance in that area, though, so that energy could have been anything supernatural. We have no way of knowing definitively what it was. Not long after that ping, the company started construction on a new house there."

The neighborhood they turned into did not look like the kind of place you would find a ghost. The new construction and green lawns appeared too bright, clean, and modern to be harboring any ill-tempered ghosts.

It only took a couple of turns until they pulled into the driveway of a two-storied, white house with dark blue trim. The three ghost hunters got out of the van with Snow, Cadence, and Sam right alongside them.

"Should we grab the gear?" Derrick paused by the back door of the van as he asked the question, his hand hovering just over the latch.

"I don't know that we'll need it. This is just supposed to be initial interviews," Aiden said and looked at Lauren.

Lauren took a moment, looking at the house. Her eyes narrowed, and she frowned. "Bring it. Just in case."

Aiden and Derrick nodded and opened the back of the van, each bringing a case. Aiden also grabbed a camcorder from one of the other bags and made sure it had battery life. He shrugged at the other two. "I figure we should record the interviews, see if we get anything in the background while we're talking."

"Good thinking." Lauren nodded.

Mrs. Owens must have seen them in the driveway because, as they turned to the house, she was in the now open front doorway. Snow noticed that the woman looked only a few years older than Cadence but was more comparable physically to Lauren. She had some weight on her and was curvier than his partner. The messy bun that her dark hair was haphazardly pulled into let wisps of loose hair fly into her face with the breeze. There were also dark circles of sleeplessness beneath her dark brown eyes. Her arms were hugged to her even though it wasn't cold, and she greeted the approaching threesome with a thin nervous smile.

"I'm so relieved you don't have any advertising on your van. I was so afraid of what the neighbors would say," she said with an apologetic smile. "Come on in. I have lemonade, iced tea, coffee, soda, water, whatever you like." She closed the door behind them hurriedly.

The three shared a look between them at Mrs. Owens' rush to get them in and concern over what others would think. They followed her down a short hall that let out into the large kitchen and breakfast area. The ghost hunters declined the offered drinks and sat down at the large kitchen table.

Looking around, Derrick noticed how incongruous the setting was to what they did. He was used to old, dirty, abandoned places. Not a new, nicely decorated, bright family home. But there was no denying that something was wrong, given the woman's obvious lack of sleep and the way her hands shook as she tried to sit down without spilling her coffee.

Snow turned to Sam and Cadence as the breathers got settled. "I'll go check out the home. Please stay with Lauren in case someone or something from our side wanders in."

"Sam's got them here. I can go with you to help check the place out," Cadence said.

Snow shook his head. "No. I know you're back, Cadence, but I would much rather you stay where it is relatively safe for right now." He held up a hand to stop her as she opened her mouth to speak. "I am not saying that I don't trust you and I am not saying that I think you are any less capable of performing your duties than you were before the Overton incident. I am simply saying that until you are fully healed, no limping or tenderness, I would prefer you to stay out of harm's way."

"He's right, sis," Sam said, backing Snow up.

Cadence frowned, her eyes narrowing a little as she considered arguing with them. She ended up relenting and nodding in agreement with them after giving it some thought, however. They were probably right, and she knew Ramon would back them up, too, if he were here.

Sam nodded to Snow, then turned his attention to the table of living people. He moved a little closer to Lauren since that was who he had a connection to. Sam watched the room like a bodyguard as he listened to the conversation between the four at the table. Cadence watched her brother, and as much as she was perturbed at being sidelined in the "safe" area, she was proud of Sam and how seriously he was taking his new duties.

"It's a beautiful home," Lauren said, starting the conversation with a compliment. "How long have you lived here?"

"About eight months or so," Mrs. Owens answered with a nervous sigh.

"When did you first have an idea that something strange was going on?" Aiden asked. He had the camera on, facing Mrs. Owens as they talked, recording the conversation.

"It all started about a month ago. It started small. Things would go missing. A glass flew off the shelf when I had a cabinet open and smashed in mid-air right in front of my face. And we always hear footsteps running up and down the stairs, or up and down the hall."

Mrs. Owens paused and took a deep breath. "What really caught my attention was when Ava suddenly started talking and playing with someone who wasn't there. A little girl who she said was named Emma. At first, we just figured it was normal growing-up stuff, you know? An imaginary friend. She's at that age." She shrugged and took a sip of her coffee.

"What made you suspect that this Emma was more than an imaginary friend?" Aiden asked.

"We took Ava to the fair one night. The condition for going was to clean her room, so we knew it was clean because we had checked it before leaving." Mrs. Owens paused, staring down into her coffee for a moment. "When we got back home, her room was a mess. It looked like a bomb had gone off in there. We took pictures..." she trailed off as she fished her cell phone out of her pocket. She fiddled with it for a moment, then set it on the table, pushing it toward Lauren and Aiden. "There, just swipe right to see them all."

Aiden picked up the phone and held it so he and Lauren could see. Derrick got up and moved to stand behind them so he could see the pictures, too. Mrs. Owens hadn't been over-exaggerating. It did look like a bomb had gone off. Toys were thrown everywhere. The sheets and blankets were off the canopy bed. The pillow was in the middle of the room, with its stuffing ripped out and thrown around. Posters had been torn from the wall, leaving fragments of paper attached to the wall with pushpins.

"Wow," Derrick said in a hushed voice. "That's ... incredible."

"And powerful," Lauren said, looking back up at the worried woman. "When were these taken, Mrs. Owens?"

"Call me, Robin, please. These were taken a week ago. Ava said that Emma had done it. That she was upset that we had gone without her. Then Ava said the strangest thing."

"What?" It was Derrick who asked, leaning forward a bit, captivated by the story.

"She said that Sarah had tried to stop Emma, but that Emma was stronger." She lifted her dark eyes from her coffee to look at the three of them. "I'm scared. I have no idea who this Sarah is that was trying to stop Emma. That was the first I had ever heard of her. But this Emma is becoming a real problem. I hope you can help us."

"What did your husband have to say after you found Ava's room destroyed like that?" Lauren passed the phone back to Robin as she asked.

"Things had been weird in the house before that, but they were all little things. Glasses falling off shelves, chairs moved, the television turning on or off by itself. They were things that my husband tried to explain away or make excuses for. But this." She tapped her phone screen. "This is when he finally admitted something was going on. This was when he agreed that we had to find someone to help us."

"How have things been since that night?" Aiden shifted in his chair a bit as the air conditioning came on and he found himself in a chilly draft.

"You're not alone," Sam said to Lauren, who jumped a little at his sudden intrusion.

For his part, Sam was now keeping a close eye on the little girl at Aiden's elbow, who was looking curiously at the camera. Most of her brown curly hair was hidden underneath a white bonnet, and a full white apron covered a dark blue dress that seemed to match her eyes. She put a hand on Aiden's arm, and he shifted again. The girl smiled, appearing to take delight in making the grown man uncomfortable.

Lauren looked from her side, where she heard Sam, to Aiden. "Why are you squirming?" she asked, not wanting to let on just yet that Sam had said something.

"Sorry, I must be under an air vent, got cold," he said.

"Uhh, bro," Derrick said, looking up, "there isn't a vent there."

Robin looked between the three of them, fear beginning to cloud her features. "Is she here?"

"Yes." Lauren closed her eyes for a moment. "She's curious. And mischievous. I don't sense any malevolence though..." She trailed off as she got lost in thought, trying to sense more about the spirit.

The girl looked over at Lauren and lost interest in the camera, beginning instead to walk toward the psychic. Two steps were all she took before Sam stepped forward, moving in between the girl and Lauren.

"That's close enough," he said to the girl.

The girl canted her head to one side and regarded Sam as if trying to puzzle him out. Her eyes narrowed for a moment, then she turned around and swiped the camera off the table. It fell to the floor with a loud clatter that made Robin jump in surprise, spilling her coffee. The little girl darted out of the room with a laugh as Aiden and Derrick moved to get the camera.

Meanwhile, Robin was grabbing napkins out of the square container she had them in at the center of the table. She was almost in tears as she frantically tried to wipe up the spilled coffee. Lauren rose and began to help Robin, putting her hands on the young mother's.

"Don't worry, we're going to help," Lauren said. "You don't have to be scared anymore."

"Was that her?" Derrick asked as Aiden waved him off, wanting to inspect his camera for damage. "Was that Emma?"

Robin and Lauren had amassed a wad of coffee-soaked napkins in front of them. Robin looked over to Derrick as she grabbed them all and began walking to the trashcan. "I think so." She threw out the used napkins and came back to the table, sitting down as Aiden set his camera back up. "I mean, I know Ava said there were two, but all I've ever heard about was Emma."

"Has Emma ever tried to physically harm you, your husband, or Ava?" Lauren asked.

"No," Robin said, shaking her head, a few more wisps of hair falling from her messy bun. "Never."

Cadence looked over as Snow came back into the room and went over to him. "The child ghost is real. She came in here and tossed the camera off the table when Sam wouldn't let her near Lauren. She looked like an old spirit, like colonial times or something."

Snow nodded slowly. "She's not alone; there is another girl's spirit here as well."

"Should we get Bethany? Help them cross over?" Sam hadn't moved from Lauren's side as he asked the question.

"It doesn't call for that yet. You forget Sam; our job here isn't to help every ghost cross over. It's to help keep the afterlife a mystery and not a proven thing."

"Says the man who has proven to them that we do exist and that there is an afterlife," Sam argued. "Besides, what about Irene Woods? Cadence told me you guys called Bethany in to get the old woman to cross over."

"Mrs. Woods was a different case," Cadence explained. "She hadn't realized she had passed, and she was becoming increasingly more violent to the living because of her confusion. She needed to move on because if left on her own, she was going to hurt someone."

"And you call that peaceful?" Sam gestured toward where Aiden hit "record" on the camera again.

"Not peaceful, no," Snow said with a sigh. "But not dangerous either. There is a fine line we walk here, Sam. I can understand your desire to take action, but it isn't called for yet."

Sam looked frustrated but nodded in acceptance of Snow's order. His lips pressed into a thin line, and he looked down at the floor, shifting his weight from one foot to another. His silent moping was disturbed, however, when the spirit of a different girl came around the corner from the family room into the kitchen.

"Who're you?" she asked as she stood at Sam's elbow, looking up at him. Her black hair was in tight natural curls beneath a white bonnet that was a stark contrast to her dark skin. Her dress had patches on it and looked like it was made of a rougher material. Her apron had no ruffles or frills like the other girl's had.

Sam knelt down and smiled at the girl. "I'm Sam. Who are you, sweetie?"

Cadence smiled a little, unable to keep the wistfulness from her expression or her heart. Her brother would have made an amazing teacher or father. Sure, they had finally, after a decade, apprehended the killer. But it still hurt at times to glimpse the man he could have become had he lived.

"Sarah," she said, her voice quiet and wavering, showing her uncertainty and nervousness. She glanced from Sam over to Aiden and his camera. "I'm sorry that Emma threw things."

Snow watched from a couple of feet away, keeping an eye out for the other ghost girl, but not seeing her. Aiden, Lauren, and Derrick were still involved in their conversation with Robin.

"Sarah, what are you doing here?" Sam asked.

"She won't let me leave," the girl said, her voice as well as her face portraying the sadness she obviously felt at this.

"Who won't let you leave? Emma?" Sam frowned in concern as he asked the question.

The girl turned to look behind her suddenly, as if startled. "I have to go." She turned and disappeared.

Sam frowned once more as he rose from his kneeling position. He walked over to Snow. "What do you make of that?"

"I'm not sure yet," Snow replied. His brows were drawn together, and Cadence could tell that her partner was not particularly happy with whatever was going through his mind.

"Thank you, Robin," Lauren said as she rose from her chair at the table. "We'll go over all of this and do a little more research. We will probably need to meet again with you and your daughter. We'll need to ask her questions about her friend."

"Right." Robin sighed in resignation. "I have to be honest, a part of me was hoping you all would come in here and tell me nothing was going on, that it was all my imagination. I was hoping this was all something that could just be explained away."

"I can understand that. But I do have to say that, in my opinion, you do have something supernatural going on here," Lauren said.

The look of defeat was unmistakable as it crossed Robin's face. "I understand. I'll tell my husband, and we will be in touch about a time that is good for you to come back."

Aiden closed up the camera as he stood. "If we come up with any other possible explanations in the meantime, we'll be in touch. And if something happens, if Emma decides to throw another tantrum like in those pictures, feel free to call us."

"Thank you," Robin said with a weak smile to all three of them.

CHAPTER 6

The Calm Before the Storm

"**Y**ou know, we really need a way for them to be able to contact us," Cadence said as they sat back down in their office.

Snow paused in sitting as he heard Cade's suggestion and then finished the movement. "You want a way for living paranormal investigators to contact us? I do believe such a thing flies in the face of what we are actually here to do," he chided.

"Not really." She shrugged her shoulders. She ran a hand through her loose honey-blonde hair, getting it out of her face as her jade-colored eyes were fixated on Snow. "Before, when we were just beat cops, so to speak, yeah. I'll give that to you. It would have been a crazy thing to suggest. But we're this new unit now, right?

Testing out how we can all work together to subvert all the weird shit that has been ramping up. We work with Aiden and Lauren just as much as we work with Whitfield and Bethany. Sure, we have people monitoring the haunted sites and such, but these guys are on the front line with the breathers. We wouldn't have known about the Irene Woods case if that one woman watching the monitor hadn't caught that they were at a house."

Snow narrowed his eyes a little as he thought over her words. His partner wasn't entirely wrong, but at length, he shook his head. "We cannot have them directly contacting us, Cadence. However, there is a solution."

"Oh?"

"Your brother." Snow smiled. "He's with Lauren constantly now. If they go on any investigations, he can contact us and make sure we know about it. You and he will just have to keep in good contact with each other, and I have little doubt that will be a problem."

Cadence nodded after a moment of thought. "You're right. I hadn't thought of that. I guess I'm just not used to him being there yet."

"Considering you just found out about the new assignment yesterday, I am hardly shocked. For all I know, Sam's connection with Lauren could have been something facilitated by others higher up to help us with exactly this issue," Snow said.

"You mean Croft?"

"No, although it could be something he suggested." Snow realized he had just opened a can of worms. He shifted in his chair a bit, uncomfortable at the knowledge that this was going to lead to a whole conversation about things he really didn't like to discuss.

"So, who is over Croft, then?" Cadence canted her head to one side and put her feet up on her desk as she asked the question. To an outsider, it would have looked like she was lounging. In reality, it was a thinly veiled effort to get her feet up off the floor. They were hurting. "Or if not his direct superior, who is it that would have that kind of authority, to make that call, to make that connection? While we're on the subject, Croft had mentioned earlier about a changing of the board. What does that mean?"

"Cadence," Snow said with a light sigh as he pinched the bridge of his nose. "We have a few long days ahead of us. I'm not sure now is the time to get into all of that."

"You've been putting this discussion off for months. Since the day I got here, in fact. If now isn't the time, Ozzie, then when is?"

Snow's sigh of resignation was loud in the quiet room. "Fine, you win. As I told you before, there is no real right or wrong religion; they all say roughly the same thing and breathers embellished from there."

"I remember you telling me that." Cadence nodded.

"We have a kind of governing board made up of deities here, a council of sorts. They are the ones that Croft reports to, and they are the ones who likely would have made the arrangements for your brother's connection to Lauren," Snow continued.

"So, what was that about the board changing?"

"Well," Snow said, "I'm sure you can understand that because of the different belief systems throughout the world and throughout history, there are a great many deities. Seven are chosen at random to serve on the council."

"Seven? Serving the religious needs of the whole world, living and dead?"

"Indeed," Snow said with a nod.

"When do they change out?" Cadence asked.

"Once a century."

"So, the ones on the council now have been serving for just over twenty years?" Cadence was thinking, processing the bits and pieces of information together. Snow loved to watch her mind work, but he also feared it a little, too. Sometimes, her answers to problems were a bit too uncanny or a little too outside of the box for his comfort.

"Yes," Snow said.

"So, the change out before this past one would have been in 1900, correct?"

"Yes," he said again with a nod.

"That makes sense then, since Overton was working on this plot in the twenties, and Wolf is connected to it as well, which means Bethany's murder, Sam's murder, all of it has been in service to this crazy scheme."

"I agree with your thinking. It would seem this group thinks that this non-human creature, the Shaldoxz that Overton was trying to summon, is the true key to accelerating their plans. And, of course, the key to releasing Shaldoxz is a great deal of blood."

"So, while we're helping with the Owens case and the TV prison show case, we also need to be doing work on trying to figure out who this person called Wolf is. Obviously, he is in contact with someone from this side, someone higher up on the food chain. If we can figure out who it is on our side that is orchestrating this, we can stop them."

Snow nodded. "I agree, and I hope that we are able to do so. It will likely take all of us working in tandem once more to resolve the situation, however."

"Yeah, well, right now, we have other priorities to focus on," Cadence said. "Are we bringing Whitfield in on any of this? The Owens or prison cases?"

"I will contact him tomorrow to see if he will have time for the prison case at the end of the week," Snow said. "I wasn't able to contact him the other night. Plus, I don't see any need to take him away from his NHD work for what seems a simple haunted house case. The NHD has been keeping him quite busy of late."

Cadence nodded and yawned. "Well, since the excitement for the day seems to be over, I think I am going to go home and rest. You would think after sleeping for five weeks, I would be wide awake, but for some reason, I am still exhausted."

"I can imagine you are," Snow said as he rose from his chair and walked over to her and she stood as well. He enveloped her in a hug, and after a moment of bewildered stiffness, she hugged him back. "I am glad you are back and doing so well. Now go, get some rest." He released her from the hug and moved back to his desk.

"Aww, missed me that much, huh, Ozzie?" Cadence grinned at him. She was quite touched at his gesture, but there was no chance that she was going to let it go by without giving him hell for it.

For his part, Snow lifted one eyebrow and shook his head. "Go home, Cadence."

Cade grinned and wiggled her fingers in a little wave at him before teleporting out of the office.

Just as she vanished, Whitfield walked into the office, looking tired and harried, as seemed to be his norm these days. His wavy ginger hair was disheveled, and he looked as if he hadn't slept in some time. He stopped and blinked just inside the doorway, as if not quite believing what he had just seen.

"Was that—" he began.

"Yes," Snow said with a smile. "Detective Riley has rejoined us."

"Oh, good! How is she doing? Is she back to work or just up and around?"

"Back to work," Snow answered as the man sat at his desk in the office. "I have to say I am surprised to see you. We understood that NHD had you buried under a mountain of work."

"They did," Whitfield said with a sour look. "I think Croft must have come up and said something. They took a bunch of stuff off my desk and told me to finish up a couple of projects by the end of the day. I just finished a little while ago. I figured I would check in here before heading home."

"Excellent timing. We'll likely need your assistance with the Barrington Prison case," Snow said.

"Barrington Prison?" Whitfield's eyebrows shot up in surprise.

"Yes. You know of it?"

"Yeah, it's not a good place. You will need me. Is that where the television show is going? There is some very nasty stuff there," Whitfield said. Snow had apprised Whitfield of the fact that a ghost-hunting television show was coming to town. Both men had been afraid it would be just them handling it. Although Sam had tried to fill in for his sister as best as he could, he wasn't Cadence.

"Yes, that is where the television show is apparently set on investigating," Snow replied.

Whitfield sighed and cradled his chin in his hand. "Hmm … I'll have to think about the best way to approach this."

"Why don't you sleep on it? Then you can advise both Cadence and me tomorrow morning," Snow suggested.

Whitfield nodded and rose. "I'll see you in the morning. G'night."

Cadence opened the door to her apartment and was greeted by the sight of Ramon on her couch. He was not in his white orderly uniform, which he had also adopted as his "doctor" clothes at the hospital. Instead, he wore black slacks and a short-sleeved, button-down shirt. He smiled as she closed the door.

"Wow," Cadence said. "I'm not used to seeing you out in the wild like this."

"Out in the wild?" He laughed a little at her phrasing. "Your apartment doesn't look like a jungle or the Serengeti to me." He watched her as she crossed the living room to him, noting her limp.

"Okay, granted," she said with a chuckle as she sat down on the couch. "I'm just so used to seeing you at Lexington. And now, I guess, the hospital," she added with a shrug. "And you're not in uniform. I've only seen you out of it once." That once had been the date they had shared prior to the shit hitting the fan with the college dorm case and Overton.

"I do get time off," Ramon said, slipping an arm around her. "I don't have to be always at the hospital like I did at Lexington. And I can dress out of uniform."

"If it means I get to come home and find you here like this, I'm not arguing," Cadence said with a smile.

"I hope you don't find it too presumptuous," Ramon said, the manners of his time and upbringing showing. "Your brother let me in to wait for you. I had come here hoping to find you already home."

"Yeah, Snow and I were trying to figure out how best to handle the upcoming case," she said. "Cases, I suppose," she amended, putting emphasis on the plural.

"Is it the television show case that Snow had mentioned?"

"That's one of them, yes," she said with a nod, her dark gold hair falling over her shoulder.

"Do you know where they are going yet?" Ramon was worried about Lexington. He knew it was in good hands, but a television show tromping through there would be rough on the new monitor. Although Ramon knew that Cade could keep Ruby pretty well-behaved, he would rather his old home not be featured on a show for all to see.

"Barrington Prison," Cade answered, closing her eyes for a moment. She changed the mental image of herself to be without shoes or socks and in pajama shorts and a sweatshirt. When she opened her eyes, Ramon's were closed. With a grin, she swung her feet up across his lap.

"Barrington Prison? I don't know it," Ramon said, his eyes still closed but a pinkish hue visible on his cheeks. His cheeks may have been pink, but the tips of his ears were flaming red.

"Oh my God, you're too adorable. You're blushing!"

"Cadence," Ramon said, clearing his throat and opening his eyes. "I am just not ... used to the familiarity."

"I just figured, knowing you, that you would want to check out my feet and legs, how they held up today." That was part of the reason she had done that. Another part of her just wanted to see how he would handle it. She knew he liked her. Their date had proven that. It had also proven that despite her arguing against it, she liked him. But if they were going to be a more regular "thing," then she wanted to see how he would deal with more modern couple behavior.

"Oh!" His ears burned even more, thinking he had misunderstood the situation, and she felt slightly bad for torturing the poor man. "Yes, of course." And just like that, he went into clinical mode, examining the scars on her feet and legs.

"Ramon?"

"Yes?" He looked up from her feet to her eyes.

"I really wasn't looking for another examination," Cadence confessed. "I just wanted to get comfortable. I've never actually had you in my home before. I like you being here, and I was just teasing you a little."

"Apologies, mi amore," Ramon said. "I'm not quite used to this yet, either. So how bad does this Barrington Prison place look to be?"

"It's not the greatest," Cadence admitted. "Prisons aren't exactly known for well-behaved people, let alone well-behaved ghosts. We've been there a couple of times for check-ins, I think. I'm not really sure how often; so much of the beginning of this life is a blur to me now.

But I do remember the monitor for the place, and I have to say I don't care for him much."

"Why?"

"First impression? He's a sexist asshole," Cadence said.

"Are you perhaps being a little harsh?" Ramon asked. "He could simply be a product of his time."

"Maybe," Cade said with a shrug. "But then again, maybe not."

"So, it's a dangerous place with a monitor you dislike. I wonder how many stitches it will take to patch you up this time."

"None if I can help it," Cade said, shaking her head.

"You are beginning to have something of a track record." Ramon smiled.

"To be fair, I've had a few weird cases," Cade protested.

"True, but if this place is so dangerous, I could just go to Croft and Snow and say you aren't ready for something this big yet."

"You wouldn't dare," Cade said, her eyes wide in surprise that he would think to pull such a ballsy move.

"Wouldn't I?" Ramon was teasing her, and the smile on his face gave him away.

"No," Cade said with a smile, narrowing her eyes a little. "You wouldn't. Because you just called me 'mi amore' a little while ago, which is the first time you've said that out loud. And I'm pretty sure you're not going to risk pissing me off now that you know I noticed."

Ramon stopped smiling and dropped his eyes for a second. "Cadence," he began, but he didn't get to finish. She leaned in and kissed him softly, putting an end to the verbal sparring.

"I liked 'mi amore' better," she whispered after breaking the kiss.

CHAPTER 7

Meet The Dead Show

The hotel the television show personalities were staying at was a five-star hotel, complete with the exclusivity and elegance that accompanies such a rating. Aiden entered the restaurant attached to the hotel and felt under-dressed in his button-down shirt, tie, and jeans. One glance at Lauren and Derrick told him that they felt just as uncomfortable despite both having dressed better. Derrick had actually worn a suit, which had astonished both Aiden and Lauren. Neither of them had known the young man even owned one. Lauren had dressed to the nines, with a cocktail dress, heels, make-up, jewelry, the whole shebang. Aiden knew she didn't get dressed up like this often.

Sam hovered around the trio, an unseen presence. He noted one spirit near the bar, and the two nodded at each other in acknowledgment. Sam had no idea if the ghost was a spirit of the restaurant or there for one of the patrons or workers, and he wasn't leaving Lauren to go find out, either.

The maître d' looked Aiden up and down with blatant condescension in his expression. "Reservations?" he asked, holding a pen over the notebook on his podium.

"We're here to meet with Attic Noises Productions," Lauren said as she interposed herself between Aiden and the man. "They're expecting us."

The man gave the three of them another look down his nose, then sighed and led the trio into the restaurant. Sam took a better look around as they walked. The walls were paneled in a dark wood that not only matched the flooring but the woodwork on the tables, chairs, and booths, as well. Each table had a candle in a honeycombed-style glass holder, and wall sconces of frosted glass emitted a low, romantic light. That low light reflected off the ceiling, which had been tiled in burnished copper, each tile having a design in relief on it. They followed the man through the restaurant to a scarlet velvet curtain, which the man pulled to one side and gestured for them to enter. "The VIP area," was all he said. Once they were through, he let the curtain swish closed behind them, once more obscuring the area from the curious looks of other diners.

"Hey! Now the party can start," a male voice said from across the room. Long legs made short work of the space between them, and he was in front of the trio, extending his hand to shake in moments. He matched

Aiden in height and build, but he had a thick head of black hair and was clean-shaven. "I'm Liam. It's nice to finally meet you."

"I'm Lauren." She shook the offered hand. "This is Aiden, and this is Derrick." She introduced each in turn, and they nodded as their names were said.

"And I'm Tina, but everyone calls me Teeny," a woman said as she stepped forward. It was obvious why everyone called her Teeny; the woman couldn't have been over five feet tall and might have weighed ninety pounds soaking wet. Liam and Teeny were rocking the modern goth look with dark hair, dark clothes, and lots of silver jewelry.

After the introductions and handshakes were done, the group ambled back to the table and took their seats. A waiter came out of a concealed door in the back of the room and took drink orders, making sure everyone had their menus. Liam took that opportunity to order one each of every hors d'oeuvres on the menu for the table.

"You must be starving, man," Aiden said with a smile.

"This dinner is on the production company's dime, bro. Live it up. Order whatever you want. Don't leave hungry or sober." He laughed and picked up his own drink, making a salute with it, and Teeny giggled.

"I drove." Aiden shrugged. "So, I'll stick to Coke, but they can drink for me."

"Good man!" Liam slapped Aiden on the back congenially.

"Seems to be quite the party for a business meeting," Lauren said with a confused smile.

"Our producer, Russell, could turn a bachelor party into a business meeting." Teeny rolled her eyes. "I swear, I have never met anyone who's so much of a stuffed shirt."

"She hasn't met Snow," Derrick said under his breath. Aiden caught what he said and laughed.

"I missed that, man. What'd you say?" Liam looked at Derrick as he asked the question.

"Oh." Derrick grimaced a little bit, embarrassed that he had actually spoken it out loud. "I was just saying that we know someone like that."

"Don't worry, guys, don't worry," Liam said. "We will get down to business, but we might as well eat and enjoy ourselves; get to know each other a little better first, right? After all, we're going to be traipsing around some old, broken-down prison together soon." He gestured to the table as the waiter brought out his tray full of drinks. As the waiter left the VIP room to go check on the first round of appetizers, Sam saw the ghost from the bar area enter, coming through the curtain without so much as ruffling it. Once more, the two of them locked gazes and nodded at each other before the spiritual stranger turned his attention to the table of breathers. Sam's curiosity got the better of him, and he made his way over to the ghost in the suit and fedora.

"Hey kid, how ya doin'?" the man asked, his speech giving away his New York origins.

"Good, thanks, you?" Sam said.

"I'm perfect, kid, thanks for askin'."

"I'm Sam."

"Joe," the ghost replied, shaking hands with Sam briefly before returning his attention to the table of breathers.

"So, which one of them is yours?" Joe looked back over at Sam as he asked the question.

"Lauren, the larger of the two women," Sam said.

"Most women would be considered larger than that little girlie over there." Joe laughed. "I hear tell that these guys are doing some kind of television show. That true?"

"Yeah." Sam nodded. "But the officers of the area already know and are preparing for it."

"Good thing. Is it true they're plannin' on doin' the prison? Barrington?" Joe bumped his fedora up a bit as he scratched at his forehead, then settled it back in place again.

"Yeah," Sam answered. He turned from the table of breathers to face Joe fully. "So, are you a resident here, or are you following one of the TV guys?"

"Neither, kid," Joe replied. "I'm just a messenger."

"A messenger?"

"Yeah. If I were you, I would see what I could do to get them tv folks to do their show somewheres else. Barrington ain't no place for the livin' no more," Joe warned, his dark eyes finally turning from the table to regard Sam as he spoke. "I ain't kiddin', kid."

Sam narrowed his eyes for a moment. "You said you were a messenger. Who is the person sending the message?"

"Does it matter, kid?"

"It might," Sam said with a nod. "I know about a few people who might have some things to hide if Barrington somehow fits into their plans."

"A few people, huh?" Joe said with an amused grunt. "You got quite the imagination, kid."

"What am I imagining? Someone sent you with this message, so clearly, there is something there that someone doesn't want discovered," Sam defended. He debated calling Cadence and Snow, but figured he would keep that on the back burner for now. He wanted to talk to this Joe more and find out what he could.

"Yer lookin' in molehills for dragons, kid," Joe quipped. "Barrington is dangerous. I know the guard there, the monitor, whatever you call 'em. He told me he heard a rumor people were gearin' up to do some kind of big investigation. He asked me to see if things were negotiable-like. If they might be amenable to goin' elsewheres."

"Like where?" Sam canted his head to one side a bit, curious as to where this was going.

"They got lotsa places with spooks 'round here, kid." Joe laughed. "It ain't gonna take 'em a lot of searchin' to find someplace else. Barrington is dangerous. Hell, kid, I know the guard, an' even I won't set foot in that place beyond the damned gates."

"If you're not from there," Sam questioned, "how do you know the monitor?"

"Jesus, kid, you are stubborn." Joe chuckled and shook his head. "Look, I've said my piece. I don't mean you or your people any harm; I'm just passin' on a message. It's on you if you wanna ignore it or not." Joe gave a shrug and turned. He paused at the curtain and looked back at the table, then at Sam. "Good luck, kid, whatever you decide." Joe then disappeared.

Sam frowned and moved closer to the table to see how things were going. The appetizers had been delivered and were being picked over pretty well, as everyone seemed to have a plate in front of them with a little bit of everything. The waiter brought another round of drinks to the table, refilling glasses where he could, or bringing new drinks entirely.

Dinner eventually began to wind down, and talk of past experiences turned to talk of the upcoming one.

"I suppose for this to be a business write-off, we should talk some business." Liam sighed as he set down his drink. "Tomorrow is the Barrington investigation. It's going to be long, two days."

"I thought you guys shot in one night?" It was Derrick who asked the question.

"No, it takes two days," Teeny replied. "The first day we go in, take a look around, and do the prep interviews with people like you. The second day, well, night really, is the actual investigation."

"And we want you guys in on the investigation, too," Liam said. "So, we'll need you both days."

"We've got this really cool experiment we're going to run during the night investigation," Teeny said, her face lighting up with excitement as she smiled. "If it works, it is going to blow all the current scientific conventions regarding paranormal research out of the water!"

"What is it?" Aiden asked.

"It's a surprise for now," Teeny answered. "We'll show you and explain it to you on-site the night of."

"It is scientific." Liam tried to reassure them. "No séances with candles and Ouija boards. Teeny designed this herself based on many of the prevailing theories in paranormal research."

Lauren kept herself from frowning, not wanting to seem ungracious to their hosts, but she had a bad feeling about this so-called experiment. She worried about the ghosts they knew, and Sam, and what this experiment might mean for them.

"You are aware that Barrington can be a lethal place, right?" Aiden looked at Liam as he asked this, trying to make sure the man wasn't all party and personality and no caution.

Liam sighed like a teenager being told something by their parent for the ten-thousandth time. "We know. Old building, we need to watch for all the usual signs of structural failure, especially in the dark. Have a little faith, man. This isn't our first rodeo."

Aiden wanted to add more but decided to save it for later. Liam seemed to be in too much of a party mood to seriously broach the dangers of the building they had chosen to investigate.

"Fine, but I have one more business question for you," Aiden said.

"And that would be?" Liam asked.

"Do you even believe in the ghosts you hunt?"

"That's not business." Liam smiled, saluting Aiden with his glass before taking a drink. "That's personal opinion."

CHAPTER 8

Barrington Prison

The mid-morning light was bright and undimmed by clouds. The ground was covered with patches of snow that seemed to sparkle under the sunlight. The wind was cold as it blew through the yard and whistled through the broken panes of glass in the windows of the prison. The dark brick edifice stood stalwart against the efforts of the encroaching nature, whether it was the grass or the wind. All windows had bars in front of them, whether they had any glass left in the panes or not. A tall brick wall topped with a great deal of rusted barbed wire stood as a silent guard around the prison and its outside areas.

Snow, Cadence, and Whitfield arrived on the front steps of the prison with the barred double doors in front of them. The crumbling parking lot behind them remained empty except for the weeds breaking through the pavement here and there. The breathers had yet to arrive. It didn't take long, as it never seemed to, for the building monitor to appear.

Roy Pruitt looked to have been in his late forties when he died. He had been a little on the stocky side, but not really out of shape. He had dark brown eyes, shaggy black hair and a trademark big, full, 1970s mustache. He wore his guard uniform, but Cadence had no trouble whatsoever imagining him being more comfortable in a polyester leisure suit, complete with some ridiculous gold chains or a medallion.

"Mornin' officers. What can I do ya for?" Roy had an easy smile and a country twang to go with the question.

"Mr. Pruitt, you remember my partner, Riley, and myself, I'm sure?" Snow asked.

"Of course, of course." The guard nodded. "Seems ya brought more company today, though."

"Yes, this is Agent Whitfield, an NHD agent." Snow introduced Whitfield to the former prison guard. "The three of us are working together as a kind of experiment for the powers that be. We'll be working here with you for the next couple of days."

"Couple of days? Somethin' goin' on?"

"There's to be a full-scale paranormal investigation here, complete with television cameras," Snow replied.

"Television cameras!" Pruitt exclaimed. "What for?"

"Ghost hunting has become popular lately," Cadence explained. "I know you've had some small teams come in here before."

"Yeah, yeah, that we have. Always managed to steer 'em clear of the worst parts of this place, though," Roy assured.

"Well, it's gotten popular enough that there are now television shows that focus on investigations into haunted places. One such show has contacted a local group, and they'll be investigating here over a few days."

"Well, shit on a stick." Pruitt frowned. "Guess people'll watch anythin' these days."

"You're not too far off there," Cadence agreed.

"It'll be fine," Snow assured the man.

"Mr. Pruitt," Cadence began.

"Ah, honey, call me Roy. Mr. Pruitt is my dad."

Cadence did her best not to bristle at being called "honey." "Okay, Roy, you had mentioned something about keeping previous investigators away from hot spots? What hot spots do you have here?" She already had a good idea, as she and Snow had gone over Croft's map and notes the night before, but she wanted to hear Roy explain it.

"Well, we have places that have a bunch of spirits, but after dark, there's somethin' worse 'round here in a couple of places. I do my best to keep the breathers out of those places if they come round after sunset."

That piqued Whitfield's interest. "What do you mean 'something worse'?" he asked.

"Just somethin' worse." Roy shrugged. "Darker, y'know? Never been able to tell who it is, though. It wears different faces, sometimes."

"Is it a non-human?" Whitfield pressed.

"One of them monsters? No." Pruitt shook his head. "Back in the eighties, we had a team come through here.

They went into one of them places and got attacked by the dark. I didn't know it was as strong as it was. That it could do what it did. After that, I've been doin' my best to make sure no breathers go to those places after dark."

"I thought day or night didn't matter," Cadence questioned, looking at Snow.

"Sometimes darkness can give power to certain specters, especially the kind that isn't really a ghost at all," Snow explained.

"What on earth does that mean?" Cade asked.

Whitfield took the explanation over. "Sometimes, especially in places like this, something can form that isn't a real spirit or a non-human creature. Places like this contain a lot of traumas—deaths, fights, rapes, regrets, anger. The passion from these emotions and acts of violence can lead to a shattering of human souls. The person's soul may have gone on but left bits behind, like debris in a house after people move out and leave what they don't want behind. The scattered bits and pieces of all these different people can come together and form something that has the intelligence of a human, but all the negativity of those violent instances."

"So, it's like a spiritual version of Frankenstein's monster, made of violence and anger?" Cadence clarified.

"That's one way to put it." Snow nodded.

"Well, we have two of the suckers here," Roy said. "There's one that keeps itself to the gallows and one in the rec room. We all do our best to keep the breathers out of there when they come by and stay the heck out of these beings' way any other time."

"You said something had happened in the eighties," Cadence questioned. "What happened?"

"In the rec room. Whatever it was y'all are callin' it, attacked a couple of people that were tryin' to make contact with the dead. Stupid idea if ya ask me, comin' into a place like this an' tryin' to contact the dead, stirrin' up God knows what." Roy turned to the side and spat before continuing his answer. "Anyways, these two got more'n they bargained fer. One of 'em got tossed clear across the rec room. Other one got a couple of pipes lobbed at his head. The one that got tossed, they had to carry him on outta here. I think he broke his back the way he landed."

"Have these specters attacked any of the spirits here?" Whitfield asked.

"No, but it ain't like we give 'em cause to neither," Roy answered.

Cadence sighed and looked at Snow. "Looks like we'll have our work cut out for us after the sun goes down then."

"I'm sure we'll be able to come up with some sort of game plan once the crews get here and we see what they have in mind for filming." Snow shrugged. "Anything else we need to be aware of, Roy?" he asked, turning back to the mustachioed prison guard.

"We got a bunch of unruly folks in the cafeteria," Roy Pruitt answered. "They like to prank the breathers."

"Prank them?" Whitfield asked. "How?"

"Touching mostly." The guard shrugged. "Yelling, poking, hitting, things like that."

"In other words, nothing we can't handle." Snow nodded.

The sound of crunching rocks and the hum of an engine drew the attention of the group of unseen ghosts toward the cracked pavement of the parking lot.

Aiden's van broke the relative silence of the cold, crisp morning with a high-pitched squeak as it stopped. Once the engine was silenced, the doors opened, and Aiden, Lauren, and Derrick exited the vehicle, as well as Sam. Cadence's limp was still very evident as she and Snow crossed the overgrown grassy area to the parking lot, leaving Whitfield to discuss particulars with Roy.

"So, how did it go last night with the TV show people?" Cadence asked as Sam walked over to her and Snow.

Sam frowned. "It went okay, but something weird happened."

"What happened?" Concern instantly colored Snow's voice as he asked the question.

"There was a ghost at the restaurant last night called Joe, or so he said. He looked like he had stepped right out of an old mobster movie. He claimed to be a friend of the monitor here, but not an inmate or former guard or anything," Sam explained. "He said I needed to try to warn them off from investigating here. That there was something evil that could hurt them."

"Did this Joe give any reason for his desire to inter-fere?" Snow frowned, thinking as he asked.

"He said he was just delivering a message for the monitor here." Sam shrugged.

"He couldn't have been." Cadence shook her head. "Mr. Pruitt only just found out about the television show when we arrived today."

"That we know of," Snow said with a look at Cadence. "Either way, I am not sure I like what's afoot with all of this."

"What do you mean?" Cadence tried to brush some of her dark blonde hair out of her face as a gust of cold wind blew the long hair from her ponytail into her face.

"We have an independent spirit, not tied to the prison nor the restaurant, it seems, approaching Sam to sway the group to go elsewhere." Snow began to tick off points on his fingers. "This independent spirit somehow knew where to find them and that Sam would be attached to them, so he had another spirit to give his warning to. This independent spirit also claimed to be a friend of Mr. Pruitt's and was delivering a message on his behalf. We also have Mr. Pruitt himself professing to be unaware of the television show until this very morning. So, either Mr. Pruitt is lying about not knowing about the show, or this Joe is lying about where his message is coming from. Neither alternative points to anything particularly positive."

Cadence looked over at her brother. "Did you pass the message on to Lauren?"

"No," Sam said with a shake of his head. "I couldn't see how doing so would really make any difference. It's not like Lauren is in charge of where a television show has set up to shoot. And it isn't like the TV show guys can change their production spot on a whim, with all the hoops they have to jump through with permits and permissions to be able to film someplace."

Both Snow and Cadence nodded, but it was Snow who responded. "A sound decision, Sam; good work. Why don't you let Lauren know we're here?"

Sam nodded and made his way back over to the trio of breathers, who were standing around outside the van, hands all firmly stuffed in the pockets of their coats.

Their breath was visible in the cold of the morning, and Derrick was hopping up and down a little to try to keep warm.

"It's not like they don't have our numbers. They could have called if they were going to be late," Aiden was grumbling as the ghosts approached.

Sam reached toward Lauren but didn't quite touch her; it was as if he were feeling her aura. "Snow and Cadence are here," Sam said.

"Snow and Cadence are here," Lauren repeated what Sam had told her to Derrick and Aiden.

"Well, at least the dead are on time," Aiden said with a sigh of notable relief. "I'm not entirely thrilled with these TV folks."

"Really? We couldn't tell," Lauren said, the sarcasm dripping from her tone.

Derrick laughed. "No kidding."

Aiden sighed and took a moment to pull his knit cap down a little on his forehead. "Look, that party boy attitude of his last night was worrisome. This place is not going to tolerate someone like that. This place is dangerous, and you have to be on your toes here, or you could get hurt."

"We know what to watch for, and where to avoid," Cadence said. "We'll help you as much as we can."

"I'm sure Cadence and Snow know what to watch out for and can help us avoid some of the nastier places," Lauren reassured.

Aiden narrowed his eyes for a moment as he looked at Lauren. "Okay, where's the pod?"

"What do you mean?" Lauren countered.

"I mean, six weeks ago, we had to cajole you into helping out on the Woods case," Aiden said. "In the last month, though, it seems like you have not only come to terms with your powers, they are growing. You realize you just told us that Cadence and Snow were here without the use of a crystal or the ghost box or my little felt cutouts? In all the time I've known you, you have always been uncomfortable with your gifts. Now you're relaxed as hell about them. What gives?"

Lauren pressed her lips together for a moment as she thought. "Well, you are right; my gifts have been growing. But I also have a spirit guide now, who can help interpret things for me that before I could only feel and have to try to figure out on my own. I think my gifts have been able to grow because I have been able to relax about them. I'm safe. I know I'm safe, even if there are other spirits around."

"A spirit guide?" It was Derrick who asked, still hopping up and down to try to stay warm in the late January cold.

"When did you pick up a spirit guide?" Aiden asked.

"Like you said, about a month ago."

"What, right after the whole college fiasco?" Derrick stopped hopping up and down for a moment.

"Yes." Lauren nodded. "And before the interrogation goes any further, it's Sam. Cadence's younger brother who helped us out during that."

"Really?" Aiden was surprised, but it also made sense since they were all so interconnected at this point.

"I'm glad Sam is with us," Lauren said as she looked over at the prison. "I've already got a bad feeling about this place."

Whatever anyone else had been about to say was cut off when a full-sized van blasting loud music came revving up into the parking area. The van was black with an electric blue design of a ghost on its side. Monster wheels held the carriage of the vehicle far above the ground as the enormous tread plowed through the gravel before coming to a stop. Shortly after the vehicle stopped, the roaring engine stopped as well, cutting off the music. Liam could be seen in the driver's seat, with Teeny in the passenger seat.

"That is a professional ghost hunting team?" Snow asked, aghast at what he saw.

"That's who they met at the restaurant last night," Sam said with a nod.

"Here we go," Cadence muttered.

CHAPTER 9

An Interview with Derrick

The group of ghost hunters, both the normal and celebrity variety, made their way up the crumbling path to the front door. Liam was carrying a couple of cases, and Teeny had a couple of tripods under her left arm. Aiden and Derrick were helping them carry gear as well. They stopped near the front of the prison and set the cases down, prompting Aiden and Derrick to do the same.

"Okay," Teeny said, "What we're going to do now is interview your researcher. Derrick, right?"

Derrick nodded and stepped forward. "Yes."

"You've got all your info down, right?" Teeny asked as she guided Derrick to the right of the large, still-locked doors.

"Yes, I do," he said with a nod. Neither Lauren nor Aiden had any doubt in their younger partner. He was great with the information and research side of things.

"Okay, you stand here," Teeny instructed. "Give us a few minutes to set up a couple of cameras."

Liam enlisted Aiden's help. One camera was at Derrick's side, angled to record Teeny, and the other was at Teeny's side, angled to record Derrick. Liam then set about rigging up the lighting.

"So, I'll stand here, ask you questions about the history of the prison, any interesting facts or encounters people have had, that kind of thing. We record from both sides at once, so we'll be able to edit it together when we get back to the studio," Teeny said, explaining things to Derrick, who nodded.

"Oh, what's the name of your group, anyway?" Liam asked as he worked on getting everything set up.

"Uh, well ... We've never really named it," Aiden answered, looking at Lauren with a shrug.

"We'll need a name to call you guys," Teeny said. "Might want to huddle up and figure it out pretty quick."

"I'd like to avoid being called ghost hunters," Lauren said, crinkling her nose a little. "I've always disliked that term."

"Hmmm..." Aiden looked to the ground for a minute, thinking. "How about Southern Paranormal Investigations? Could go with SPI for short?"

Lauren thought about it for a moment and nodded. "Yeah, that sounds good."

"Cool, there's the name then," Liam said with a grin.

Liam double-checked the angles on both cameras and that they both were recording, as Teeny helped

Derrick clip a mic pack on before doing her own. Liam gave her a thumbs-up, and she nodded.

"We're here with Derrick Getty, the youngest member of Southern Paranormal Investigations and their team researcher. Derrick, we're standing here outside of Barrington Prison. What can you tell us about it?"

Derrick took a breath to steady his nerves and began. "Barrington Prison was built in 1940 and remained in operation for less than half a century, closing its doors for good in 1985. This is where the area sent the worst of its criminals. The death sentence was enforced here, and rather than upgrading to the electric chair or lethal injection, Barrington Prison kept it old-fashioned. There was a dedicated gallows building in the same yard where the prisoners would have their exercise time. So, every day when they went outside, they were faced with death.

"In the early days, the first few wardens of Barrington used to have the prisoners line up outside, rain or shine, to watch a soon-to-be executed inmate's last walk from the prison to the gallows building. That practice stopped when a riot occurred that killed not only prisoners, and ironically the man that was to be hung, but also the medical examiner and some attendees of the execution. That was in 1954.

"This was a prison; it doesn't have a quiet history. There were murders, rapes, attacks, and other than the riot I just mentioned, there were two other major incidents. The first was in 1968. A prisoner overpowered a guard in the rec room, and some prisoners barricaded themselves in there, demanding more humane conditions. Apparently, some of the guards were notorious for their mistreatment of the inmates. It took about nine hours, but the warden and other officers diffused the situation. Or so they thought. When they entered the rec room, the errant guards and some of the less-than-popular inmates were found stripped, hanging from the overhead pipes by their bound wrists, and they had been mostly skinned. There were seven deaths in total at that time. Two were guards, and five were other inmates."

Teeny couldn't hide the look of shock and disgust on her face at that. "Oh my God," she murmured.

"As I said, these inmates were the worst this area had to offer." Derrick gave Teeny a bit of an apologetic shrug before continuing on. "The second riot happened less than a decade later in 1975. This one occurred in the cafeteria and was stamped out by the guards pretty quickly, but not before there were deaths. No one seems to know really how or why, but a fight started. It only took about 45 minutes for the warden and his guards to regain control, but that was plenty of time for blood to be shed. Three guards and eight inmates died that day.

"As newer prisons with better security measures opened, Barrington became less used. When the state did away with the death penalty, Barrington's doors were closed for good."

Aiden was impressed. He'd heard Derrick give information and results of research before. But the way Derrick had effectively crafted it into a story to tell for the cameras was fantastic, and he hadn't missed a beat. No stammering, no skipping, no nervousness. As excited as Derrick could get in the moment with evidence, he was as cool as a cucumber with history.

"Derrick, thank you," Teeny said, coming out from under the spell Derrick had cast with his storytelling.

"That is an incredible history. So, not only do we have the state-mandated deaths from the gallows but also three riots that caused many violent and gruesome deaths, on top of the usual attacks, assaults, murders, and illnesses that would normally occur in a place like this."

"Yes," Derrick said, nodding in agreement. "I've never been inside myself, but I've heard it's not a great place to go exploring or investigating."

"Why do you say that?" Teeny asked.

"Because you aren't the first team to investigate here," Derrick answered. "In my research, I found that there was a team that entered in 1985, not long after it closed down. They were working for the *Ripley's Believe It or Not* television show. A crew of four went into the prison to shoot a segment of the show to be aired in a later episode. There was one sound guy, a cameraman, and two investigators. Rumor has it they were investigating the rec room, the site of the goriest riot. The only thing for certain is that two of them walked out unharmed, one was carried out after his back was broken, and the other walked out but died a few days later from an aneurysm which was likely due to the concussion he received here. The sound guy went crazy and was committed to an asylum less than a week afterward. The television show never ran the segment."

Teeny paused, stunned by what she had just heard. "Well, maybe we'll skip the rec room tonight then," she said at length with a nervous smile.

"Cut," Liam said in a loud voice, which made Teeny jump a bit.

"Is all that true?" Teeny asked as she leaned into Derrick. "Or was it just for the cameras?"

"No, it's all true. I can get my laptop and show you the sites I went to for research if you want," Derrick offered.

"No. No, that's fine. It just ... It makes this investigation a bit creepier," she said.

"Which is why it's going to be awesome," Liam said, giving a high five to Derrick. "Dude, I couldn't have asked for a better story. You were phenomenal."

"Thanks," Derrick said, looking a bit uncertain. "It wasn't a story, though. That all really happened."

"Well, here's hoping a few decades have chilled the ghosts out then, right?" Liam smiled.

Snow turned to Roy, who was with the spirits gathered around the breathers as the interview was taking place. "How was that incident with the breathers in the rec room allowed to happen? Were you the monitor then?"

"No, sir, I wasn't," Roy said. "In fact, that there mess is what got the old monitor yanked from his position and got me my promotion."

"Who was the old monitor?" Cadence asked.

"One of them guards killed in the '54 riot," Roy said. "He'd been the boss here fer a while. I ain't sure what happened. I tended to keep to the cafeteria myself. But I do recall when all that happened. It riled up everyone inside."

"I don't suppose you would know if the inmates left have anything planned for these folks, do you?" It was Snow who asked this, concern creasing his brow. The last thing he wanted was for there to be trouble during this investigation, especially trouble that caused as much harm as the rec room incident.

"Hell, most of 'em prolly don't even know this is comin,'" Roy said. "They can be quick on their toes when they wanna be, of course, but I doubt most of 'em are gonna have much to do aside from maybe some pranks. Nothin' hurtful just touches an' whispers an' the like. We ain't gotten much in the way of visitors since that incident; maybe once or twice a year we'll get a ghost hunter or a couple of teenagers lookin' fer a place to canoodle. I can usually get rid of 'em pretty quick, though."

"What about the rec room?" Cadence asked.

"After what happened, we done our best to make sure that room is inaccessible. No one in or out," Roy said. "Course, if they are determined, the breathers could try to get in. Ain't like we could brick up the doorway. We done our best to block it off, like I said, and we've managed to keep folk out."

"What about the darkness that's in there?" Whitfield had been fairly quiet up until he asked that question.

Roy shrugged. "It don't come out of that room. Same for the one in the gallows. Not sure why, but they keep to the rooms they're in. That's why we stay away from 'em and why we try to keep any breathers that come around out of 'em."

"Well, hopefully, these people will be easily swayed away from the dangerous places," Snow said.

"I'm not so sure Liam thinks this place is dangerous," Sam posited.

"Oh?" Snow questioned. "What makes you say that?"

"Maybe I'm wrong." Sam shrugged. "But Aiden seemed to get the same feeling that I had. Like Liam was just in this for the TV show and the party. Teeny seems more into the actual reason that they're here.

She says she has some big experiment going tomorrow night; that, if it works, will supposedly rock the scientific world in regards to paranormal research."

"Sam, honey," Cadence said, shaking her head, "I know you are new to all of this, but that is definitely something you should have led with."

Sam made a sour face and shook his head. "Cade " Snow cut him off before he could say any retort he had in mind.

"Both of you cut it out," Snow scolded. "There's been a lot going on this morning. The point is, we know now. Did she say what the experiment was?"

"No, she said she wanted to keep it a surprise," Sam said with a sigh.

"Well," Whitfield said, "Here's hoping whatever she has up her sleeve isn't too problematic."

"Okay," Teeny said as she unclipped Derrick's mic. "Let's move this inside for the rest of the interviews."

CHAPTER 10

Inside the Prison

As they neared the door, Teeny produced the keys from her pocket and flashed a grin at the group. She was obviously excited to begin, as was her partner. The other three, especially Aiden, had their reservations. The key took a little coaxing, as the lock was not in the best condition. With a deafening screech of protest, the mechanism gave way, and the door opened.

"Ha! I win," Teeny crowed to the laughter of her partner as she got the door unlocked. It swung inward on its hinges, with the usual creaks and squeaks of a disused door.

Roy appeared next to Teeny, not that she saw him, and frowned. "Did my damnedest to keep that thing from openin' up," he said to Snow and Cadence.

"Well, that racket had to have woken the dead." Liam smirked.

"That may not be the reaction you want," Aiden said, looking into the lobby area of the prison, trepidation obvious on his face.

"No shit, Sherlock." Roy shook his head. "These folks are a special breed of stupid, ain't they?"

"Once we get in, we will get cameras rolling, and you can tell us what has you so damn spooked about this place." Liam gestured for everyone to enter the building.

They filed through the door into the long, rectangular lobby. There were orange plastic chairs, some with holes in them, strewn about the small area, none of them in the upright position. Dirt and dust were covering the floor, as well as the security counter in front of them. Across the room from the front doors was a hallway that went through the thick-barred security door and into the prison proper. The wall to the left had two doors, both closed. The single door on the wall to their right was open, and a wall of old metal lockers was visible. Natural light came in from the barred windows on either side of the double front doors and from a large domed skylight in the ceiling. Frost and a light dusting of snow still clung to the glass on the roof, diffusing the light and making it softer.

"How on earth did that thing stay intact?" Lauren wondered aloud as she looked up at the skylight.

"Maybe the ghosts kept it together," Liam said with a laugh.

"Oh, Mr. Pruitt," Snow said as he walked alongside the prison guard, "Do you know any spirit by the name of Joe?"

Roy stopped and looked at Snow, then pursed his lips as he thought. Cadence thought the expression made him look ridiculous with his lips drawn in so tight beneath that huge mustache of his.

"That's an awfully common name," the monitor said after a few moments of thinking. "There are a couple of Joe's in here."

"No, this would have been an independent spirit," Snow corrected.

"Independent?" Roy was confused by the term about a ghost.

"He wasn't from here, but he wasn't tied to where I met him either," Sam clarified. "He said he knew you and was delivering a message for you?"

"Oh yeah? What was the message?"

"That I needed to try to get these guys to find someplace else to investigate," Sam said.

"Huh," Roy grunted. "I didn't even know people were comin' till these two showed up this mornin' an' told me." He gestured to Snow and Cadence.

"Are you sure? This Joe guy looked like some kind of 1940s mobster, complete with fedora and New York accent," Sam explained.

"Now, I am sure I don't know no one like that," Roy assured him.

"Quite curious then," Snow puzzled with a frown.

"According to the blueprints I pulled up online the other day, the visitation rooms are through that far left door." Derrick pointed them out. "That's the security station in front of us. The guard rooms, locker room, and break room would be over there on the right. This door on the left here is the warden's office."

"Think there would be anything back there?" Liam asked, looking over at the trio of locals.

"Most of the violence and deaths took place in the prison proper," Derrick explained.

"The cafeteria, the rec room, showers, the cellblocks themselves," intoned Liam. "Then, of course, out in the yard and death row." He looked over at Aiden pointedly. "See, your boy there isn't the only one who does his homework."

Lauren stayed back near the front door, and Sam was at her side. The color had drained from her face, and her eyes were wide.

Sam touched her aura gently. "Shield yourself. I'm right here. Just wall yourself off from it for now."

"Lauren," Aiden said, noting his friend's apparent alarm. "What is it? Are you okay?"

"Yeah, I'll be okay," she whispered, her voice subdued. "Just nasty vibes here, is all. The atmosphere in here is just the heaviest I think I have ever encountered."

"That's called dust," Liam joked.

"Save the drama for the cameras," Teeny said as she and Liam went about setting up the tripods and cameras for the interviews.

"Seriously?" Aiden questioned, anger flashing in his eyes as he turned to face the two television ghost hunters.

"You want us to fawn all over her because she has a bad feeling? Do you have any idea how many times we have heard that from so-called psychics?"

"So-called?" Derrick asked, the anger spreading in him. "Are you kidding me? You have no idea what she is capable of. We do."

Snow turned to Sam. "See if you can get Lauren to calm them down. The last thing we need is their anger feeding into this place, which is likely what is intended."

"Where the hell is Roy?" Cadence asked, noticing the monitor had disappeared from the lobby room. "Shouldn't he be trying to keep this place in check?"

"Whatcha think I been doin', little lady?" Roy asked as he appeared beside her. He gave her a wink and a smile. "The noise of the door openin' and the livin' bein' here has the folks in the back all riled up. They're tryin' to influence the livin', make 'em fight fer their amusement."

Lauren nodded a bit at Sam's whispered words and took a deep breath. "I'll be okay, really. I just needed a minute to adjust to the atmosphere."

The smirk that Teeny and Liam shared between themselves did not go unnoticed by Aiden, who opted to mentally count to ten instead of hitting something. Liam found two chairs that seemed as whole as possible and set them upright in front of the cameras, taking a rag from his back pocket and dusting the chairs off. Teeny turned on the bright lights affixed to the top of the camera to showcase where Liam was setting up the chairs. The little red light on one of the cameras was already on, indicating that it was recording. Teeny moved over to Lauren, and the older woman stood still, letting Teeny affix the microphone to her shirt and clip the battery pack to the back of her jeans.

"Okay, so since Lauren is a little bit wigged out, why don't we do her interview first so that she can step out if she needs to afterward," Teeny suggested as she led Lauren over to the lit area.

Lauren nodded and moved toward the two chairs, taking a seat in one of them. Teeny's mic pack was still on, as she had never bothered removing it after Derrick's interview. Teeny then took her seat in the chair next to Lauren as Liam took his position behind the other camera. Sam stayed out of the range of the cameras, just in case, but was close enough to protect Lauren from any spirits out to play tricks or pranks on her.

"We're here with Lauren Kurtz, the ex-wife of Dan Kurtz, who had investigated this prison previously with another member of their local ghost-hunting group, Southern Paranormal Investigations. Lauren, thank you for being with us today."

"Thanks for having us," Lauren said calmly, though she could feel her heart beating a mile a minute.

"Why did you not come with your ex-husband when he and Aiden Perkins investigated here? Was it because of the divorce?"

"No," Lauren replied. "Our divorce was, for the most part, amicable, and both of us remained with the paranormal group. I'm a psychic, medium, whatever term you want to use. Because of my abilities and sensitivities, Dan and Aiden often went to check out locations before I went in. In this case, they came back and said no way."

"Why did they say no?" Teeny asked.

"You would probably do better asking Aiden that. They didn't give me much of a reason beyond it being a more dangerous place than they had anticipated. I left it at that because I trusted them."

"Now, Lauren, when we entered today, you said you had doubts about this being a good idea. Why?"

"There is a lot of anger and bloodshed here, and I can feel it. I've been in places with pain, bloodshed, anger, all those negative feelings and emotions before. But this place … it's different. It seems like it is magnified here. It has a dangerous edge to it."

"Do you know much of the history of this place?" Teeny asked.

"I know what you know, what Derrick told us. But before this, no, I hadn't known much of the history other than it had some problems in the 80s right around the time it closed down, and that there had been riots here," Lauren said with a bit of a laugh. "I knew about as much as most of the regular public, probably. But I usually like to go in knowing as little as possible about the history of a location we're investigating. I don't want prior knowledge coloring anything I might see or hear."

"You're saying you see and hear ghosts, then?" Teeny continued the interview.

"I hear them often if they wish to talk to me. Seeing them is … it's not like I see you sitting across from me. It's more along the lines of flashes in my mind, feelings that I know are not mine, images, memories, things like that."

"Are you prepared for what you might see and feel on this investigation?"

"I'm not entirely sure I am, but I suppose we'll find out, won't we?" Lauren smiled a little, trying to shake the feeling of dark, venomous clouds gathering around them.

"Now Aiden is here, as is another member of your group, but I have to ask, where is Dan?" Teeny knew the answer, but she had to get it on camera.

"He died last year," Lauren's voice became terse.

"Is it true that his death was related to an investigation you all were doing?" Teeny asked.

Both Aiden and Derrick stepped forward in defense of Lauren. "What the hell kind of question is that?" Aiden growled.

"A legitimate one." Teeny looked up at Aiden but didn't move from her seat. "A very legitimate one, considering he and you are the only two with any practical knowledge of this prison and its hauntings. Was his death in any way connected to this place?"

"Dan died of a heart attack in his apartment. He did not die in any location we were working on," Lauren answered. She stood and unclipped the mic pack they had outfitted her with. "And I am done answering your asinine questions." She tossed the pack on the chair and headed out the front door, Sam going with her.

"Good for her," Snow said approvingly. "These two television people are horrid. Who would ask such a question?"

"People who go for the shock value of their show instead of actually being interested in furthering paranormal research," Cade replied. "Which on the one hand is sad but on the other hand is great for us. They aren't going to dig deep enough to come up with anything we likely have to try to cover up."

Snow turned to Roy. "Is there anything that can be done about the way this place is encouraging anger? Aiden is usually quite level-headed, not prone to the kind of outbursts we are seeing here."

Roy shrugged. "Not sure I can do much more about the atmosphere here. But I'll see if anyone is still tryin' to stir up trouble back there." Roy turned and disappeared.

"I want to make sure Sam and Lauren are doing alright," Snow said. "Are you alright here with Aiden and Derrick?"

"I'm not made of porcelain, Snow. I'm not going to break, I promise. Ramon cleared me. I'm fine to be here," Cade reassured.

"Well, that's not going to stop me worrying over you now, is it?" Snow said with a smile. He then followed Sam and Lauren out.

"Dude, what the hell is your issue?" Aiden asked Liam as Cadence turned her attention back to them.

"Look," Liam said, putting up his hands in a defensive gesture. "I have no issue with you guys, and neither does Teeny. We have to ask these questions. People were going to wonder why we didn't have Dan here on the show since you and he were the ones who investigated this place before. Now they know why, and they can see that Lauren is still broken up about it. Trust me; it will play well."

"I'll go apologize once we're done here," Teeny assured him. "I really wasn't trying to upset her."

"Your questions sure were phrased badly then, if upsetting her wasn't your goal," Aiden resentfully grumbled. "You guys knew ahead of time that Dan had died. I was at the shop when you were on the phone with her a few days ago, telling us you had moved up your schedule."

"That wasn't us, man. That was Russell," Liam defended. "And yeah, he told us Dan died, but we had to get the answer on camera, as well as the fact that his death had nothing to do with this place. Otherwise, the viewers will wonder."

"I'm sorry I upset her," Teeny apologized. "But if I'm going to get this mic on you, you need to sit. You're a foot and a half taller than me."

Aiden sat down and let the small woman go about clipping the mic to him. Once done, she took her seat opposite him.

"Aiden Perkins, thank you for joining us here at Barrington Prison today," Teeny started.

"Thanks for having us," he replied, his voice and manner calm, in contrast to just a few minutes ago.

"You have investigated this prison before, right?"

"Yes, but it wasn't a full-scale investigation. We were more checking it out to see if we should or could do that here," Aiden said.

"Right, you and Dan, the man who was with you, determined it to be too dangerous for your group to proceed with a full investigation, as I understand. What made you decide this?"

"It just seemed to be a bit too much. I'm no psychic, but even I could feel the oppression and the anger here," Aiden explained. "We came in, and it was like trying to walk through sludge. The feelings were a bit much for us, and neither one of us is nearly as sensitive as Lauren."

"Other than the feelings of oppression and anger, did you get any evidence here?" Teeny asked.

"We got noises, things that sounded like cell doors opening and closing. When we were in the hall by the kitchen, it sounded like there was a huge fight going on inside, but when we got inside, there was nothing." Aiden shrugged. "A few touches and scratches once we got in there, but no fight."

"What are the places you would warn people to stay away from in here, and what are the places you think we might have the best luck investigating?"

"Cellblock one held the worst of the worst in here when the prison was in operation. That was the direction from where we heard the cell doors opening and closing. It was also used as both death row and solitary confinement. The kitchen might be worth investigating since that's where the 1975 prison riot that killed eight prisoners and three guards took place. I would warn people who don't know what they are doing to stay away from the rec room and the gallows building outside. The rec room had a lot of debris in front of the door, like someone was trying to barricade something in there. We did go outside to the gallows, but we didn't go in. Dan and I both got horrible feelings out there, so we decided to go with our guts and stay out."

"You didn't go in?" Teeny reiterated. "I'm a little surprised that a ghost hunter would avoid a place so steeped in death as a prison gallows."

"Well, first, it wasn't a full-scale investigation; we were just scouting. And I'm not sure if I can explain it the right way, but it just didn't feel right. It felt like if we went in there, one or both of us were going to get hurt."

"Have you ever had that kind of feeling in any other place?"

"No, never." Aiden shook his head.

"How many places have you investigated?"

"More than I can easily count off the top of my head," Aiden answered.

"Have you ever been hurt or attacked in any of those other places?"

"Oh, there have been scratches and things like that. Things that tend to go with being a paranormal investigator. But even in places where we have been attacked, it has never felt that dangerous. There was just this feeling that if we stepped in there … one, or both of us, might not walk back out."

"Alright, thank you, Aiden." Teeny reached forward, shaking Aiden's hand.

Liam turned his cameras off as Teeny helped Aiden get the mic pack off him. Silence fell on the group as Derrick hung back, unaware of Cadence standing right beside him. Liam began taking the tripods down and setting them by the door.

"Hey, Aiden," Liam said, offering a camera to the man. "Would you want to help us out?"

"What do you need?" Aiden took the camera in hand as he replied.

"Film Teeny and I doing our intro outside, and maybe a thing or two in here," Liam said with a shrug.

"Yeah, sure." Aiden wasn't sure he wanted to help them out that much after the way they had treated Lauren. "Hey Derrick, go check on Lauren, will you?"

"Sure," Derrick said with a nod and turned, slipping out the door.

"Thanks, Aiden," Liam said, trying to smooth over the anger from earlier. "We appreciate it. Let's start outside."

Everyone walked out of the prison, and Teeny closed the prison door but did not lock it up again, since they would more than likely be going right back inside.

Teeny and Liam situated themselves on the crumbling sidewalk, a little bit before the couple of steps that led up to the prison door. Liam got his mic pack snapped on and looked over to Aiden.

"Start with a wide shot, get the prison in, then slowly close in and center on us," Liam said. "Got it?"

"Sounds simple enough," Aiden said, trying to not be irritated by the way Liam was talking to him as if he didn't know what he was doing. He took a deep breath, then steadied himself and the camera while finding the best framing of the two hosts and the prison itself. The wide rectangular building's brick façade and iron bars over the windows were a wonderful backdrop to the ghost-hunting duo. They stood on the concrete steps of the prison's entrance, the massive front doors behind them. Once satisfied, Aiden hit "record" and gave them a thumbs up.

CHAPTER 11

Splitting the Party

"Welcome to *The Dead Show*," Liam said, speaking to the camera as Aiden slowly began to narrow the view from the prison building to the two television hosts. "Tonight, we're bringing you with us to Barrington Prison, a place that has been steeped in violence and death, even though it was in operation for less than fifty years."

"A television show once fled from this place under mysterious circumstances shortly after it closed more than thirty years ago," Teeny said. "No one has attempted a full-scale investigation of the prison since then. Until now."

"Tonight, we will take you inside these halls and give you access to rooms that haven't hosted the living in decades," Liam said. "Will we be brave enough to venture into the areas that are reputedly the most haunted and the most dangerous? You'll have to wait and see."

"Also, tonight, we will be running an experiment," Teeny said. "I've been working for a long time on this, and tonight is its maiden voyage, so to speak. If it works, we may be able to see and speak to a spirit in real-time."

Cadence frowned as she heard that. Snow had gone with the others back to Aiden's van to check on Lauren and put heads together for plans. If this experiment worked, it was not going to make their job any easier.

"So, sit tight and stay with us," Liam said. "As *The Dead Show* investigates Barrington Prison."

Liam gave a motion to cut, and Aiden stopped recording. Aiden was less than thrilled about the news of what this experiment was supposed to be able to do. He only hoped that it would fail. It was almost funny because, just a year ago, he would have been cheering this kind of experiment on, wanting it to be successful. But now, he didn't want to be responsible for having to try to hide footage from a television show.

Liam walked over and grabbed the camera from Aiden. "Just give me a minute to review this, make sure it looks okay," he said. He rewound the footage to where it began at the wide shot and watched through it. "Damn, not bad at all, Aiden. Want a job as our cameraman?"

"I'm good where I am," Aiden said with a chuckle. "Thanks, though."

"You know, between the interviews and the intro we just shot, I'm not sure we really need to do any interiors," Teeny said.

"What, you want to just leave it for tomorrow night?" Liam looked over at his partner with a raised eyebrow.

"Why not?" Teeny shrugged. "We're leaving the experiment as a surprise; let's do this show a little differently. Let's go into this without knowing the layout, other than the blueprints. No daytime shots other than what we already have."

"I have a feeling this one might be different from your normal shows anyway," Aiden said. "If what Derrick dug up is anything to go by."

"Exactly!" Teeny said with a smile. "We have the intro; we'll lead after that with Aiden and Lauren's interviews, then leave it with Derrick's history before just going to the night shoot."

"That kid does know how to tell a creepy story," Liam said with a slow nod.

"See? It's perfect," Teeny said with a triumphant smile.

"If you guys are good, I want to go check on Lauren," Aiden said.

"Yeah, sure, we'll grab our gear, lock up, and we can all get out of here," Liam said.

Cadence could see Lauren's color had mostly returned, and she looked steadier than when she had left the prison. Derrick and Snow were already with Sam and Lauren at the van as Aiden and Cadence made their way over. Roy and Whitfield followed Liam and Teeny as they went about gathering their things and relocking the front doors of the prison.

"You okay?" Aiden asked, reaching out and putting a hand on Lauren's arm.

"Yeah," Lauren sighed. "You can all stop hovering over me now."

"We're just concerned," Derrick said.

"I don't know why I let her get under my skin like that," Lauren confessed, shaking her head.

"Dan is still a touchy subject for you; it's understandable," Aiden comforted. "And the way she phrased the question was like she was on the attack or something. If she had come at me like that, I might have walked out too, and I'm not nearly as psychically sensitive or as close to the subject as you are."

Lauren smiled at Aiden and gave him a hug. "Thank you." She then turned to Derrick. "And thank you, too. I didn't mean to upset everyone."

"It's all good." Derrick smiled.

Aiden's gaze moved to Derrick. "And congratulations to you. They were seriously impressed with the history you gave and the way you gave it."

"Really?" Derrick was unable to keep the excitement from his face or voice.

"Yeah, man, they were impressed. So was I," Aiden praised.

"Me, too," Lauren echoed.

"I'm so glad," Derrick said with a happy sigh. "I was working on that for a while."

"It showed," Liam said, coming up to stand beside the group. "You guys were all fantastic."

"And Lauren, I'm sorry," Teeny said. "I should have phrased the question better, but it's just how it popped into my mind. I really didn't mean to hurt you."

"It's okay," Lauren said with a sigh. "Thanks for the apology. It's just that it's been less than a year since he died. Ex-husband or not, I still loved him, and it still hurts. And I was on edge in there anyway, so probably a little more prone to overreaction."

Teeny smiled and crossed the distance between her and Lauren with her arms outstretched, hugging the woman with affection. "We work in Hollywood. We're used to overreaction," the small woman said jokingly.

"So, is that all you needed us for?" Aiden asked, looking over at Liam.

"For today, yeah," Liam replied. "But like we said last night, I want you guys on our team while we investigate. We want you to come in with us and be special guests for the episode. You seem to be a great investigator, Derrick definitely knows his shit about this place, and if Lauren is up for this, it would be interesting to work that angle here. We don't bring in psychics that often."

"I'm not so sure about me," Lauren demurred. "Give me some time to think about it, but that place just feels evil. I'm not sure I can handle what's in there." Even with Sam protecting her, the prison was overwhelming. She was glad that Dan and Aiden had decided against it before. She couldn't imagine trying to go in there for an investigation without the help and protection Sam was giving her.

"Well, it'd be a shame to go without you, but I can understand," Teeny said.

Teeny and Liam finished packing up their van and walked back over to the group clustered around Aiden's van. "We'll be heading back here tomorrow night for the investigation. We've hired an off-duty cop to make sure none of the locals try to screw with us," Teeny said.

"I think you'd find it difficult to find many locals who would willingly come out here at all, let alone to screw with you guys," Aiden said.

"People have done it on other investigations before," Liam replied. "Better safe than sorry, right?"

"Can't argue that." Aiden nodded. "You have my number. I'll do it for sure, but I don't know about Lauren. She needs to think about if she would go in there again or not. Derrick will likely come with me."

"Sounds good, man. Plan on four tomorrow afternoon then," Liam said, reaching over to shake Aiden's hand. "We'll call if there is any change."

"It's good that they at least had the foresight to have someone here who can call for help if there is an emergency," Snow said as the breathers began to disperse. "I have a feeling this investigation is not going to be the smoothest."

"I have a feeling you're right." Cade nodded. She glanced back over at the building. Roy's presence, hovering just inside the open doorway, was not lost on her. For all of his disappearing while they were there, she was glad to see him taking his duties moderately seriously, keeping watch over the living intruders.

"Hey, Tom, how's it going?" Aiden called to the man behind the lunch counter. The smell of barbeque permeated the air, making Aiden's mouth water. Derrick and Lauren followed him in as Tom looked up, one hand holding a phone to his ear, and gave the trio a wave.

Pho-Q was a favorite place for the trio for lunch, as it was in the same strip mall as Lauren's shop. The restaurant was a mash-up of barbeque and Vietnamese soup. Tom and his business partner Chris had owned the place for three years, and it was a popular local eatery. They chose a table near the counter and took their seats, not needing to see a menu. They knew what they wanted.

"What do you mean they won't let you do the radio ad?" Tom could be heard saying. He paused and then shook his head in disbelief. "It's the name of the restaurant! That's ridiculous!"

Derrick chuckled and shook his head. He knew what the name of the restaurant sounded like when said aloud. He could believe that someone would be giving them a hard time about a radio ad.

"Whatever, fine. We just won't spend our advertising money with them." Tom hung up the phone. He took a moment to calm himself and then walked over to the table. "Hey, guys, the usual?"

"Three bowls of pho with pulled pork." Aiden nodded.

"You guys are in at a weird time," Tom noted. "Got something going on?"

"Yeah, actually," Derrick said. "You ever hear of a TV show called *The Dead Show*?"

"Haven't watched it, but I have heard of it. My wife's friend loves all that paranormal stuff," Tom said.

"Well, they are in town, and they asked us to help them investigate Barrington Prison," Lauren said. "We'll be on the show."

"Oh, that is sweet! You'll have to let me know when they're going to air it. We can have a viewing party here or something. I'll go get your orders." The man turned and made his way back to the kitchen.

"Have you decided if you're going back now that you've had a night to sleep on it?" Aiden asked as he turned his attention to Lauren.

"I have," she said after taking a deep breath. "I'm not going back. You and Dan said it seemed too dangerous a place for me. And I'll be honest, the feelings I got from that place were flat-out scary, and that was in broad daylight. I had to shield myself, and even then, the oppressiveness of the place was getting to me. And I was inside for less than an hour. I don't think I could manage to be there all night."

"Okay." Aiden nodded. "That's fair. What about you, Derrick?"

"Oh, I'm in," Derrick said with a grin.

"Just keep in touch with me," Lauren requested. "That way, I know the two of you are alright."

"Will do," Aiden said, sitting back just a little, as Tom came back with their three bowls of pulled pork pho.

Derrick looked up at Tom and shook his head. "I know that you know what the name of this place sounds like. Why do you keep trying to get radio ads? You know they won't let you."

"It's fun to rattle their chains every now and then." The middle-aged man smiled. A waitress came over and brought their drinks, setting them down with straws before scurrying off to take care of another table.

"What does Chris think about that?" Lauren asked.

"Who do you think is out there trying to get the radio ads done?" Tom said, laughing.

"The two of you are terrible, and I feel bad for your wives," Lauren said with a smile, shaking her head.

"Eh, they knew what they were getting into when they married us." Tom smiled before turning and heading back into the kitchen.

Lauren laughed and shook her head. "Terrible."

"Yeah, but damn good food," Aiden countered.

Lauren's phone rang, preventing her from digging into her pho. She looked at the number and frowned before answering. "Hello?"

Both men paused in their eating as they watched Lauren's face quickly change expression from concerned to alarmed.

"Are you okay?" Lauren's voice was sharp with worry. She paused, listening to the person on the other side. "No, it's fine. It may just be me who comes. Aiden and Derrick have another appointment. I'll be there soon. I just need to gather some things."

"What was that?" Aiden asked after she had hung up the phone.

"That was Robin Owens," Lauren replied. "Apparently, she was physically assaulted by Emma a little while ago."

"That escalated fast," Derrick said.

Aiden nodded, agreeing. "Yeah, a little too fast for my liking. Dude, I know you want to come to the prison tonight for the investigation, but I would feel a lot better if you were with Lauren. If things have gotten that serious, I don't want her alone."

"I'm not alone, remember?" Lauren was referring to Sam as she spoke.

"I know, but I still don't want you to be the only one of us there. I want a physical person there to help, not just an ethereal one," Aiden said. "I can do the prison. I've been there before, anyway."

"But then you'll be alone," Lauren said, pointing out the obvious.

"Not really," Derrick said with a shrug. "He'll have Liam and Teeny with him. And you know Cadence and Snow will be there."

"And you're fine with not going to the big television shoot?" Lauren lifted a skeptical eyebrow.

"Yeah, I'm good. I did my thing yesterday with the history. And to be honest, I'm a little scared I would slip up and say something I shouldn't," Derrick admitted. "Besides, doing a TV show is cool and all, but this is helping a family. That's more important."

"Let's finish lunch first," Aiden suggested. "Then I can help get you guys prepared to go. Then I'll head off to the prison."

Sam, hovering nearby as always, pulled out his phone and dialed his sister.

"Hey, Sam," Cadence said as she answered the phone.

"Hey, sis," Sam said. "They are splitting the party on us tonight."

"What do you mean?" His sister's voice was half confused and half concerned.

"Lauren just got a call from Robin Owens. Apparently, Emma attacked her. I don't know how bad the attack was yet, but now Lauren and Derrick are going to the Owens' home, and Aiden is going to the prison."

"Hang on a sec," Cade said. She relayed the information to Snow. Sam could hear Snow's voice in the background but couldn't make out what he was saying. After a few minutes of muted conversation between Cadence and Snow, Cadence came back to speak with Sam.

"Okay, we think we have a solution," Cade offered.

"Okay," Sam said, waiting for her to continue.

"Snow and I have to go to the prison. We have no choice, really. Whitfield will go with you. He said he had something to finish up for the NHD but that he should be able to meet you soon. Sound good?"

"Sounds good," Sam confirmed. "I'll see him when he gets there. Oh, and Cade?"

"Yeah?"

"You and Snow be careful tonight," Sam implored.

"We will be. You too," Cadence agreed before hanging up with her brother.

CHAPTER 12

The Night Begins

A iden pulled his van into the gravelly parking lot of broken cement. The van that Teeny and Liam were using was already there, the back doors open wide, though the two investigators were nowhere to be seen. Aiden killed the engine and got out of the vehicle. He knew Snow and Cadence would be here somewhere as well since the living were traipsing through a haunted building. He leaned against the door and waited, his arms crossed over his chest.

"Good timing," Liam called to Aiden with a wave as he came down the small hill from the prison. "We've got most of the equipment in already, but I'll need your help for this last piece."

"You could have called me in earlier. I would have helped." Aiden pushed off the side of his van and crossed the few feet over to *The Dead Show* van. Glancing in the back, he could see there was indeed only one thing left. A strange case the size of a large dog cage that looked as if it were made out of glass or thick, clear plastic was attached to a black base about three inches thick.

"Nah, it's all good," Liam said as he climbed up into the van and dragged the box toward the opening so that he and Aiden could carry it inside.

"Bet you've never seen anything like this." Liam smiled.

"You'd be right What is it?" Aiden helped him turn the box so that the handles on its sides were easy for them to grab.

"A ghost-catching box," Liam said.

"A what?" Aiden couldn't keep the chuckle from his voice at the ridiculous name.

"Yeah, I know," Liam said with a shake of his head and a grimace. "We haven't come up with anything better yet. We had been calling it a Faraday box, but it's a little too different from what one of those really is. This is our first field test of it."

"What is it supposed to do?" Aiden asked. Both men grunted as they got it out of the van and the full weight of it pulled on their arms. "Damn ... it's heavy."

"I know, right?" Liam's voice was showing strain from the physical exertion of carrying the heavy box. "There's science behind it. I guess Teeny is better at explaining that, though. All I know is it is supposed to suck ghosts near it inside and make them visible."

"How does it do that?" Aiden asked, feeling a knot form in his stomach.

"Like I said, Teeny knows the science it's based on. I just hope it works." Liam would have shrugged with his answer, but the weight of the box made that impossible.

Aiden frowned and glanced up at the prison. If this box did what Liam said it could do, this is exactly the kind of thing that Cade and Snow didn't need. He debated "accidentally" dropping his side in the hopes that it would break something, but the last thing he needed was a television show suing him for breaking their experimental equipment. Given the disdain and indifference the two seemed to be showing to the profession they chose to be in, he hoped that it was a gimmick. Perhaps it would just have a projector in it that would show mist or a pre-recorded figure in the box. Theatrics for a television show, that had to be it.

"Where do we have to carry this bad boy to?" Aiden asked as they got nearer to the prison.

"We were thinking of putting it in that big round open area between all of the cellblocks. That way, it is pretty central to everything except the gallows," Liam said.

"Is that a wise idea?" Aiden's eyebrow lifted as he asked the question. He had already told them that several areas had bad juju.

"Is what a wise idea?" Teeny asked as the men came into the prison. The lobby now boasted three long white portable plastic tables that had cases of equipment on them. Snow and Cadence were off to one side, unseen by the humans.

"I think Aiden is of the opinion that we shouldn't do anything near any of the so-called trouble spots," Liam answered.

"I just have no idea what this beast of a thing is supposed to do, is all. You get something violent, and it might backfire," Aiden said as he and Liam set the box down on the floor for a moment.

"Okay," Teeny said with a sigh. "What it does is send out electromagnetic pulses that should give the ghosts more energy and draw them in. This place has been left alone for a long time, so the extra energy to feed off of should make them want to follow it back to the box like a starving person following the scent of food to a feast. At that point, the box should sense the signatures of a spirit's presence. Lower temp, higher electromagnetic frequency, all those usual bells and whistles. It will then put out an opposite signal to the EMF that the ghost is putting out to pull it into the box."

"Operating on the theory that magnetic opposites attract," Aiden posited.

"Exactly," Teeny confirmed with a nod, looking pleased. "See, someone understands me." She shot a look at Liam. "Anyway, once it is trapped in the box, we barrage it with high EMF to excite particles in the box to try to make it visible."

"But high EMF can cause hallucinations in human beings. What if you just imagine that you see something, like a self-fulfilling prophecy? You think you should see something, so you hallucinate that you do."

"Hence the cameras," Teeny explained. "No matter what we think we see or don't see, we'll have a regular camera, a night vision camera, and a thermal camera trained on it, as well as a couple of audio recorders in the box to get the electronic voice phenomenon the ghost produces."

"It's an experiment." Liam shrugged. "If it works great, if it doesn't, there's no harm in trying."

Aiden nodded and shrugged. "I can't argue with that," he agreed, even though he really wanted to.

"This is concerning," Snow said as talk of the box died down, and the two television personalities began outfitting Aiden with his mic pack, GoPro camera, and such.

"You think it will work?" Cadence moved closer to the box to get a better look at it as she asked the question.

"Careful, Cadence," Snow said. "I'm not sure whether it will work or not, but it sounds as if she has done enough research to make it plausible. Where the devil is Roy?"

"He seems to go missing quite a lot for a monitor. Not that I miss him," Cade said. The guy gave her the creeps, and she wanted nothing more than to punch him in his smug, self-satisfied face.

"It does seem to be something of an issue, doesn't it?" Snow murmured.

"Something of an issue? He hasn't even checked in with us yet, Snow. I thought they were supposed to do that as soon as we got here," Cadence argued as the two of them watched the ghost hunters set up their equipment.

"They are," Snow agreed, his voice terse, painting a clear picture of his displeasure as he frowned.

Cadence stepped away from the box and limped back over to Snow. "Something is up, and with the way our cases tend to go, I don't like it."

"Under normal circumstances, I would say that you are paranoid. However, given what we've been through in less than a year, I have to admit I think you're right. I'm uneasy about this as well. How are you feeling?"

He asked the last because her limping had not gone unnoticed.

Cadence shrugged off his words and concern. "I'm fine. Well, not fine," she corrected, knowing he would nitpick at her. "I'm still tender, especially on my feet, but it isn't awful. Thanks for checking" She offered him a smile. She was working on not reacting to others' concern with anger.

He smiled back at her, and they watched the three living people set up their cameras and other equipment. Pulling out his phone, he hit a button to dial Mr. Pruitt and listened as it rang. He frowned when there was no answer and pocketed the phone after hanging up once more. In the meantime, Liam had gotten his personal camera strapped to his body and Teeny got hers secured as well.

"You have pockets or some way to carry equipment, right?" Teeny asked Aiden as she walked over to him.

"Of course." Aiden nodded.

"Good. EMF detector and audio recorder right here." She handed the equipment to him. "And here's the night vision camera you'll be using."

"What about the camera you guys just strapped on me?" Aiden poked at the GoPro camera on his chest.

"That will catch whatever you are facing. The night vision camera you can move around and catch other things around you, hopefully. That way, if you are filming to your right, but something happens in front of you, we can catch it."

Aiden hoped they didn't catch anything. For once, he wished with all his might that there would be no shenanigans from any spirits. He knew Cade and Snow had to be here, but he had no idea how he would convince Liam and Teeny to hide any overt evidence if they got any. And he wasn't in a place to be able to really ask Cade or Snow for advice either. He fidgeted a bit with the straps of the camera they had put on him to try to do something with his nervous energy.

CHAPTER 13

The Owens Home

Lauren's blue Prius made its way down the smooth streets of the neighborhood the Owens lived in. It was late afternoon, but the sun was already beginning to set as Lauren and Derrick passed new house after new house. The well-manicured lawns still had some patches of snow on them, which almost seemed to glow in the late afternoon light. Sam's presence in the back seat was unnoticed by Derrick, but Lauren was aware of him.

"Still hard to believe ghosts would be in a place like this. It's all so … clean and new," Derrick stated.

"I know." Lauren nodded her head in agreement. "But the land is old, and not all spirits are attached to buildings."

"True. Um, how do you want to do things tonight?" Derrick's voice betrayed a hint of nerves. "I mean, without Aiden here to do command."

"We'll be fine." Lauren smiled reassuringly. She knew Sam would do his damnedest to protect them. "We can do this without a command center. We have all of our equipment. The command center is really just a safety net for us, to call us on the radio if he sees something we don't, or in the more run-down places we investigate in case someone gets hurt."

"So Aiden could come out and investigate with us instead of sitting behind a computer bank all night?" Derrick questioned.

"He could, though in some places, having that safety net is nice." Lauren pulled into the Owens' driveway. The porch and garage lights were on, and the front windows were already aglow with lighting from the inside. The paranormal investigators got out of the car and moved to the back to grab the first few cases to be brought in. As they stepped up onto the porch, the porch lights went out.

"Well, someone doesn't want us here," Lauren murmured, giving Derrick a look.

Derrick made a face. "Joy."

Lauren rang the doorbell. It took only a moment for the door to be opened by a tall man with close-cropped brown hair and a goatee. He had the same dark circles under his eyes that Robin Owens had. Lauren extended her hand to the man.

"You must be Mr. Owens. I'm Lauren Kurtz, and this is Derrick Getty."

"Nice to meet you," the man greeted. "I'm Doug Owens. My wife has filled me in on what you all do. Come on in."

Sam followed Lauren and Derrick in as Doug closed the door behind them.

In the hall, it was easy to look up and see the small form of a little girl kneeling on the floor of the second story, her delicate hands wrapped around two of the balustrades of the railing that went around the stair and upper balcony area. Wavy, light brown hair framed the innocent face peering down at them. Lauren smiled at the girl and waved to her. The girl waved back, then rose and scampered back to her room.

"You have a beautiful daughter," Lauren complimented.

Doug glanced up at the balcony, then chuckled. "Yes, she is, and curious, and all those other things five-year-olds can be. Let's go to the family room." He led them down the front hallway into the kitchen and then turned right. He led them through an archway into the family room, where Robin was seated on a couch.

Robin offered them a weak smile. "Thank you for coming. I'm sorry to call you in ahead of what we had talked about before."

"It's alright," Lauren assured her. She and Derrick set their cases down. "Would you mind going to get the last few things out of the car?" she asked Derrick. He nodded and headed back out.

"You sounded terrified on the phone," Lauren said as she moved toward Robin, making sure her voice was warm, smooth, and comforting. Doug moved to sit by his wife and put an arm around her.

"This afternoon, I was doing homework with Ava at the kitchen table. She was being stubborn and didn't want to finish it. Of course, I told her she had to." Robin took a deep breath, trying to calm herself. Sam kept an ear on the conversation and his eyes on the room while Robin continued.

"Ava argued that she had to go play, that Emma said it was time to go play. I told her that Emma was not her mother, I was. That Emma did not get to have any say in if it is homework time, playtime, bath time, or bedtime. I guess Emma was there and didn't like that."

"What happened?" Lauren prompted, as Robin seemed to stall on saying more.

"All of a sudden, I was on the floor," Robin said with a shake of her head. "The chair had toppled over, and it felt like my arms had been stuck in beehives." She pushed up the sleeves of her sweater, and there were vivid red scratches up and down her arms. Some had even bled but weren't deep enough to be dangerous.

"Ava screamed and ran up to her room," Robin continued. "She came back down about half an hour later, and she was still crying. She was apologizing, sorry that she had been arguing, but that she was scared of what Emma would do if she didn't do what Emma wanted."

Derrick came back in with the last couple of cases and set them down by the others he and Lauren had brought in. He saw Robin's arms and his eyes widened, but he said nothing as he made his way over to them.

"I told her to call you after that," Doug said. "When she called me and told me what happened, sent me the photos of her arms ... I can't let my wife and daughter be terrorized like this." Despite offering comfort to his wife, his body sang with tension and anger. "I hate that I can't protect them from this."

"You were right to call us in. It seems like things have escalated since we saw you a couple of days ago. And that's understating the matter," Lauren said. "Would you be comfortable if we set up a video camera so that we can get proof of Robin's arms and record a statement of what happened? And may we interview Ava too?"

Robin and Doug shared a look between them, and Doug eventually nodded. "Why don't you guys record Robin's story," Doug suggested. "I'll go up and talk to Ava and then bring her down when she's ready."

Derrick was already beginning to set up the video camera on the tripod when Lauren interrupted him. "I've got this. Why don't you go with Doug and meet Ava? That way, she knows at least one of us when she comes down here."

Derrick looked to Doug, who nodded and waved for Derrick to follow him. Down the hall and up the stairs they went. Brightly colored construction paper covered with drawings and glitter festooned the first door on the right as they topped the stairs, indicating that it had to be Ava's room. Doug moved to the door and knocked.

"Ava, honey? There's someone here I want you to meet," he called. He then opened the door.

The room was cheerful and definitely looked as if it belonged to a girl. White wallpaper with unicorns, fairies, and rainbows covered the walls. A canopied bed to the left was bookended on each side with a nightstand that had lamps of fairies, their wings glowing. The furniture was white wood, including the many-shelved unit to the right that held books, stuffed animals, and toys.

Ava sat on the carpeted floor in front of a unique Victorian-style dollhouse that had working lights. One of the dolls was in her hand. Her dark eyes were wary as she watched her father enter with Derrick, a man she didn't know. She set the doll down carefully on the floor, then rose to her feet. She wore pink jeans and a sweat-shirt that boasted an image of the Power Puff Girls.

"Ava, this is Derrick. Derrick, my daughter Ava," Doug said, making the introductions.

"Hi," Ava said in a voice that was small and showed her shyness.

"Hi, sweetie. That dollhouse looks pretty cool. Would you show it to me?" He didn't want to approach the girl without an invitation, as she looked very skittish. Given what was going on in her home, he could understand why she would be, too.

Ava cast a glance at her father for direction, and he gave a supportive nod. Doug crossed the room and sat down on the floor next to where she was standing, so she wouldn't feel alone with the stranger.

"Come on, Punkin," Doug encouraged. "Let's show Derrick your pretty dollhouse."

"Emma says not to talk to him," Ava said in a quiet voice, giving Derrick an apologetic look. She did, how-ever, kneel back down on the floor next to her father.

"Why doesn't she want you talking to me?" Derrick asked, giving her a bright smile. "I'm not a bad guy."

"She says you are," Ava said. "She says you want to hurt her and me and Sarah. She says you are evil. She says the woman is a devil."

Doug's eyes went wide. "Woah now, Punkin, think about it. Would we let anyone in our house that would hurt you?"

Ava looked up at her father and gave him a shrug of her tiny shoulders. "I dunno," she mumbled.

"Yes, you do," Doug said. "I would never let anyone come here who would want to hurt you or Mommy."

"Emma doesn't sound like a very nice person if she is trying to make you afraid of people," Derrick said.

"I thought she was nice," the child said, her eyes showing a sadness that should never be on a five-year-old's face. "But she is mean to Sarah. Now, she's kind of scary."

"I have a friend downstairs; her name is Lauren. I think she would really like to meet you and talk to you about Emma and Sarah. She may be able to help make them a little less scary," Derrick said.

"Sarah isn't scary. She's nice. She has to do what Emma says," Ava said.

"Why?" both men asked in unison.

"Umm." The girl's brow furrowed as she tried to get the words right. "Something about ... Sarah belongs to her. So, Emma gets to boss her around."

"Sounds like Sarah needs some help, too, then," Derrick said. "Would you like to come talk to Lauren?"

"I thought you want to see my dollhouse?"

"Oh, of course. We'll go downstairs after you show me this pretty dollhouse," Derrick said, giving the girl a smile.

Ava turned to the house, picking up the doll she had been playing with before and used the doll to take Derrick on a tour of the house. She showed off the lights that worked and the intricate metalwork of the brass bed in the parents' room. The piano in the living room actually played music, and from the small attic room at the top, she showed Derrick her favorite piece. She held out to him a beautifully decorated Christmas tree that had tiny wrapped presents beneath it. After he had admired it properly, she put it in the living room and plugged it in. The tree lit up, and Ava unplugged the other lights in the small room, leaving only the colored lights of the tree to illuminate the doll's living room.

"I can see why you like it so much." Derrick smiled.

"I love it. Mommy made it for me."

"Wow, that makes it extra special then, huh?" Derrick smiled at the girl, happy that she was still able to find some solace in her make-believe play.

"Yeah!" She looked at her dad and sighed. "I'm gonna get into trouble. But let's go talk to the lady."

Derrick stood and smiled at the little girl. "Don't worry, sweetie. We're here to help you. I promise."

CHAPTER 14

Let's Rock!

"**Y**ou two ready to rock?" Liam had gotten one of the tripod cameras set up facing the table Teeny and Aiden were next to. He flipped a switch and lights came on, making it bright enough to film.

Aiden lifted an eyebrow. "We're not just going to start walking through?"

"Nah, this is TV, man. We have to introduce stuff," Liam said, pushing "record," then making his way over to them.

"Welcome back." Teeny looked at the camera with a smile after Liam had settled in on the opposite side of her from Aiden, the two tall men framing the small woman. "Night is falling on Barrington Prison, and we're about to begin our night-long investigation into this tragic location. With us tonight is our special guest, Aiden Perkins, who co-leads the local paranormal group Southern Paranormal Investigations and has investigated this prison before."

"As usual," Liam said, taking over the presentation without missing a beat, "we're well equipped with our EMF readers, temperature gauges, audio recorders, still cameras, both normal and full spectrum, and an array of video cameras, including our body cams."

"You'll be right with us as we make our way through the hallways of this once strong and stoic building. We'll be going into some areas that haven't seen the living since shortly after the prison was decommissioned in the '80s." Teeny picked up from Liam's tech talk. She then turned to Aiden and gave him a charming smile. "What do you say, Aiden? Are you ready to help us release the ghosts of this prison's past?"

"If it's safe to, then sure," Aiden replied, looking at Teeny and Liam instead of the camera. "But I still say some areas of this place are spiritually unsafe to go."

Teeny looked back at the camera, her smile only a tiny bit forced after Aiden's answer. "Is that a foreshadowing of danger? Or is it the trumped-up fears of old superstitions and legends? It's time to find out as we turn off the lights and begin our investigation."

They stood there for a moment, and then Liam moved to the camera and stopped the recording. Teeny began getting her equipment together. They waited for Liam as he took down the lights and Teeny spread out a blueprint of the building.

"I figure we'll hit the second cellblock first and then move on to the cafeteria," she said. "We'll see how long that takes us. I want to try out the box at midnight."

"Speaking of superstitions," Aiden said with a hint of sarcasm.

"Aiden, this is a television show, not a normal investigation. We have to play it up for the drama a bit," she said.

"Can't have the viewers getting too bored," Liam said, picking up a weird contraption that looked a little familiar to Aiden. "And we have to do solitary and death row as well."

"Is that an SLS camera?"

"Yup!" Liam grinned as he answered. "We probably have the budget to buy one, but I made this baby myself. Just needed the Xbox Kinect, its power adaptor, and a tablet."

"I thought Teeny was your inventor," Aiden said with a bit of a grin, making a mental note to talk to Derrick about his Xbox stuff.

"I invent the cool, edgy stuff," Teeny said with a smirk to her partner. "He gets the DIY videos off of YouTube."

"Ouch," Liam said, clutching at his chest with one hand, still holding the SLS with the other. "That hurts. You wound me." The grin on his face said otherwise.

"Yeah, yeah," Teeny said, waving his words away.

Aiden grinned. They obviously had camaraderie, having been working together for the past few years. Liam could be off-putting at times, but Teeny seemed to at least have a genuine interest in what they were doing. The sound of an engine caught Aiden's attention, and he turned toward the doors of the lobby.

"That your off-duty cop arriving?" He looked between Liam and Teeny as he asked this.

"Should be," Liam said.

Teeny went to the doors and opened one as the figure of their guard, shrouded by the darkness outside, had his hand raised to knock.

"I take it you heard me coming," a familiar voice said.

"No freaking way," Cadence muttered, both she and Aiden moving closer as the security for the evening stepped in the door.

"I just wanted to introduce myself to you before you all begin your evening. I'm Detective Andy Halleran." He extended a hand to Teeny; she shook it with a smile of evident interest in this person in front of her.

"Detective," Aiden said as he approached them. "How are you doing? It's been a little while."

Andy blinked in surprise. "I didn't expect to see you here," he said, shaking Aiden's hand. "I'm doing well, thanks. How is … How is everyone else doing?"

"Everyone's good, thanks," Aiden said with a knowing nod to Andy.

"I didn't realize you two would know each other," Liam said.

"He and his group worked as consultants on a case a month or two back," Andy said with a shrug, not wanting to go into detail. "As I understand it, I'm simply going to be stationed outside in my car, making sure your investigation here isn't disturbed, correct?"

"Yeah, here," Liam said as he tossed a walkie-talkie to Andy, who caught it as if it had been a thrown football. "We'll be on channel 2. Radio us if you see anything weird; we'll radio you if we need help, but that's just a precaution."

Andy nodded, turning the radio on and making sure it was tuned to the right channel. "Sounds good. I'll keep an ear out for you."

"Thank you, Detective," Teeny said with a smile and a sparkle in her eye.

Andy chuckled lightly and nodded to her before turning and heading back out. Aiden closed the door behind him.

"Is he single?" Teeny asked as soon as the latch to the door clicked home.

"Are you kidding me?" Liam's voice was filled with indignation. "We're filming *The Dead Show*, not *The Bachelorette*, Teeny. Get your head together." His personality seemed to turn on a dime at Teeny's interest in Detective Halleran.

"Says the guy who has been using his pseudo-celebrity status to chase anything with a vagina that would pay attention," Teeny said, her tone a little too sharp.

"Hey," Aiden said in a stern voice. "You two want to argue about hookups, do it on your own time. It's obvious that you have some issues to work out, but this is not the time or place to do it. We need to get moving with this investigation."

Both of them looked at Aiden and nodded in turn. There was still anger and resentment visible on their faces and tension in the air, but Aiden was glad he had been able to keep the argument from escalating. The atmosphere at the prison was rife with tension and anger, which seemed to make everyone a little more hot-headed than they normally were.

"You're right," Teeny said after a moment of mentally pulling herself back together. "I want to be back here at 11:30, so we can move the box and get it all set up in time for its midnight trial. Until then, let's go explore a little." She gave a smile, and it was evident that the smile was tight—faked enthusiasm for the cameras and the two with her.

"Jesus, Snow. If they keep going like that, one of them is going to murder the other by the time this is over with." Cadence looked over at her partner, her jade eyes solemn and concerned.

"I worry about that as well. At least, in this case, Aiden's cooler head prevailed. However, as we saw the other day, that may not be something we can always count on. And where in the bloody hell is Mr. Pruitt?"

"Been in the back tryin' to see if I can get some of these nimrods to behave," Roy said as he materialized beside Cadence and Snow. "Sorry to keep you waiting, but I figured that was more important."

Snow nodded, accepting Pruitt's excuse, but Cade could read Snow's face and body language. Even he was sensing something off about the former prison guard.

"They keep you so busy back there that you can't even answer your phone?" Cadence wasn't about to let him off the hook so easily.

"Sometimes they do, yeah. They're criminals, missy. It's not like they're known fer bein' well-behaved." Roy shrugged, not letting the doubts of Cadence bother him.

"Okay," Liam said with a smile as he rubbed his hands together, his tiff with Teeny out of his mind for now, replaced by the excitement of the investigation. "Ready to get this started?"

"Ready," Teeny said, her own smile now genuine, as was her enthusiasm.

"Ready," Aiden replied, although he was far more serious and less enthusiastic than the other two.

"Let's get this show started!" Liam led the way out of the lobby and into the prison proper, followed by Teeny, with Aiden bringing up the rear. The three ghosts followed the three breathers into the dark halls of Barrington Prison.

CHAPTER 15

Ava's Story

Sam couldn't help but smile at the little girl who came in with her father and Derrick. She looked so adorable. There was a small pang of hurt in knowing that he had missed out on the opportunity to have a family through no fault or decision of his own. But that only redoubled his desire to help this family out and to make sure that the little girl here would be kept safe.

Lauren had finished asking Robin about the attack for the record, and the camera had been recording their conversation as they chatted. Both women, from their seats on the couch, looked up and smiled as the trio entered the room.

"Hey, Jellybean, come here," Robin said, opening her arms to her daughter. Ava ran across the room and happily launched herself into her mother's arms and lap. Robin hugged her close, then loosened her grip a little as Doug took a seat and Derrick took up position behind the camera.

"Lauren, I would like you to meet my daughter, Ava," Robin said. She then leaned down to speak in Ava's ear. "Jellybean, this is Miss Lauren. She's come to help us out with Emma's temper tantrums."

Ava looked at Lauren for a moment with eyes that betrayed an old soul. "How? Are you going to hurt them?"

"No, I'm not. I'm going to try to get Emma and Sarah to rest peacefully, so they can be where they should be," Lauren explained.

"Emma says this is where she's sposed to be. She lived here a long time ago. She says we have no right to be here. She says if I'm her friend, she'll let us stay. I have to be nice to her and be her friend," Ava said.

"That doesn't sound like a friendly thing to say to someone, does it?" Lauren asked.

Ava shrugged from her mother's lap at first, but then shook her head from side to side in slow motion.

"Does she scare you?" Lauren leaned over toward the girl, lowering her voice to a conspiratorial whisper.

Ava nodded. "Especially when she has fits, like after the fair or today with Mommy."

"Would you like me to help put her to rest? I won't hurt her, I swear," Lauren said.

Ava nodded again. "Yeah … if you can. I don't want to be scared."

"Oh, sweetie, you should never be scared in your own home," Lauren said. "We'll see what we can do to fix it.

But I have to talk to you a little and ask you some questions first, okay?"

"Okay," Ava said, giving another nod.

Lauren nodded back. "When did you first meet Emma?"

"I guess … around Christmas," Ava answered. "We were on break from school." The little girl's brown eyes glittered with happiness at the mention of Christmas. "I was outside playing in the snow. She was on the swing set. Sarah was there. She didn't want to play. She's always sad."

"Did you know that they were ghosts, or did you think they were real little girls?"

"I thought maybe they were real. Playing dress up. I like to play dress up. I have a bunch of princess gowns and fairy wings, and "

She was stopped by a playful poke in the belly by her mother. "Jellybean, Miss Lauren isn't here to hear about your costumes, sweetie."

"Oh," Ava said. "I thought she was real, but she walked through the back door without opening it. Mom said it was time to come in for dinner. Emma didn't want me to go."

"Did she say anything to you that time? Anything scary or threatening?"

"No, she just didn't understand. She says where she's from, kids and parents didn't eat together, 'cept maybe for Sunday dinner. She says we're interesting," Ava said.

"And Sarah, how did you meet her?"

"Emma told me her name. She didn't talk to me for a few days. She likes my dollhouse, and one time when Emma was away, Sarah stayed to play with it. We had fun. She really likes all the lights in it. They only had candle lights, she told me."

"If Sarah seems so sad being around Emma, why does she stay with her?" Lauren had already assumed why, but she wanted to hear how Ava would phrase it.

"Emma says Sarah belongs to her and has to do what she says. That's when I thought Emma might not be nice, 'cause that's not how nice people talk. People don't own other people. And acting bossy isn't very nice. When I told Emma that, she got real mad at me and said she would break my dollhouse if I didn't take it back."

"What did you do when she said that?" Lauren was trying hard not to just hug the poor little girl. She remembered how frightening and confusing being so young with these gifts was.

"I took it back," Ava said in a small voice with a shrug. "I didn't want her to break my dollhouse."

A crash sounded from the next room, loud and metallic. Everyone in the family jumped. Derrick grabbed the camera off the tripod and ran into the kitchen, where he stopped short. There had been a ceiling-mounted pot and pan hanger, and it had fallen, along with everything it had been holding, to the kitchen floor. Footsteps sounded right behind him as no one had been slow in following to find out what had happened.

"How on earth..." Doug said, trailing off.

"Emma," Ava whispered.

"Emma," Sam said. He could see the little girl in her blue dress and white apron, her dark blue eyes glaring at them from across the sea of fallen pots and pans. Small hands clenched into fists were held tight to her hips, and her lips were pressed tight together.

"I don't want you or your people here," Emma said to Sam.

"It's not about what you want, Emma," Sam said, his voice calm but authoritative.

"It is so," she said with an impatient stamp of her foot. "It's my house, my land, and I get to say who can come and go."

"I'm fairly sure that even when you were alive, it was your parents who got to say such things. Just because you are dead doesn't mean you have that right now," Sam said as Robin and Doug set about picking up the pots and pans.

"It's my family's land," Emma said, her southern twang thick.

"Your family sold this land. Your grandfather grieved the loss of you and your parents so much that he sold the land off. It hasn't been in your family for many years now," Sam said.

Lauren was standing still on the threshold between the family room and the kitchen. She was aware of Emma's presence, and though she couldn't see or hear either of them, she was aware on some level that Sam was communicating with her.

Derrick was nearby, almost on a swivel as he moved between filming the couple picking up their pots and pans and Lauren. He had no idea what was up, other than she was sensing something, but he didn't want to voice that knowledge. He didn't want to instill any more fear into this family than they already were suffering.

Ava had stayed behind with Lauren while her mom and dad cleaned up the mess that Emma had made. She remained silent for a time as she thought about something and then tugged on Lauren's sleeve.

Lauren was pulled from her concentration by that tug and knelt down next to Ava. "What, honey?"

"Is he your friend, too?" The little girl pointed over toward seemingly nothing as she asked this.

Lauren looked where she was pointing and came to a realization as she saw no one there. "Who?"

"The man with the yellow hair talking to Emma," Ava said.

"You can see him?"

Ava nodded in response to Lauren's question.

"You have a very rare talent," Lauren said. "Which might explain a few things."

CHAPTER 16

Getting into It

The lobby of the prison let out through a now-defunct security checkpoint. Past the door was a large tile atrium. There were areas of gray where tiles had fallen off in chunks. The tiles themselves had aged to the point that whatever color they had been was muted beneath the layers of grime and dust. The footsteps of the three humans echoed strangely in the domed room. There were small patches of graffiti in here and some old beer cans along the wall. These attested to human intrusion at some point, but also attested to the fact that those intrusions had been brief as well as few and far between.

There were doors off of the atrium for administration offices and for the prison clinic. To their left was a heavy locked door made of iron bars that went to cellblock two, which had been considered general population. To their right was a similar door that led to cellblock one. Cellblock one was comprised of death row and solitary confinement. Directly in front of them was yet another door of iron bars guarding a shorter hallway. That hallway led to the kitchen, cafeteria, showers, and rec room. A set of double doors at the end of that hallway led out to the yard and the gallows building, as well as the laundry building.

"Let's try the clinic first," Liam said.

"With all the sickness and trauma from riots and fights, it sounds like a good starting point," Teeny said, agreeing with her co-star.

Liam tried the door and found it unlocked. The door opened three inches and stopped, the hinges rusted.

"Anyone on that side of the door trying to keep it closed?" Cadence looked at Roy as she asked the question.

"Nah," Roy replied in his usual thick twang. "We got some residuals in there, but ain't no one gonna fight someone tryin' ta open the door."

Liam frowned after pushing a few times, then he stepped back and kicked the door hard. It budged a couple of inches. One more forceful kick was all it took to break the door's resistance. The door swung open, leaving a ninety-degree arc in the dust on the floor. The team stepped inside the clinic with trepidation.

Two metal gurneys remained, although one was on its side. The other was at a strange angle in the middle of the room. The ceiling boasted rails that had likely once held curtains, but only a few rings remained in the tracks. Along the wall to their right were floor-to-ceiling cabinets that had crosshatched wire guarding the glass against breaking. The cabinets had once held medical supplies. All that was left was a spilled bottle of iodine that had turned the shelf rust-colored ages ago.

Teeny went over to the filing cabinet that was next to what was presumably the doctor's desk. She had to yank on it but got the top drawer open. To her disappointment, the drawer was empty. She tried the other four drawers and came up just as empty-handed.

"Well, that was a bust." She sighed.

"Try the desk," Liam said. "Aiden, why don't you go over to the bed and try to get some EVP?"

Aiden nodded and made his way to the back of the clinic, where the two gurneys were. He started the recorder and put it on the gurney that was right side up. "Is there anyone here who wishes to communicate?" It was the usual beginning to an EVP session.

Cadence shook her head as the audio recorder was set down through the leg of the spirit of a patient. For his part, the patient groaned in pain, but otherwise, he didn't seem to be aware. Snow was at the other end of the room, watching over Teeny and Liam as they looked for whatever it was they were looking for in the drawers and cabinets. Roy stood in the door, his arms crossed over his chest.

The patient groaned louder, and Cadence knew it would be caught on the tape, but she wasn't worried. She would have been when she started, but she had grown more accustomed to the fact that some things were allowed. The groan was not, however, loud enough to be heard audibly in the room.

"Well, this room seems to be a total bust," Liam said. He had taken a few still pictures while Teeny had used the thermal camera.

"Yeah, I have nothing unusual here," Teeny said.

"Okay, Aiden, stop recording and we'll get out of here," Liam said. "Want to try the admin office or go straight to the cellblocks?"

"Cellblocks would probably be best. I doubt there is anything much in the administration area," Teeny said.

Aiden rejoined them, pocketing the audio recorder. "Which cellblock?" he asked.

"Let's go for two first, the general population one," Teeny said.

"Alright, let's rock," Liam said.

Their footsteps echoed against the cinderblock walls as Liam, Teeny, and Aiden walked down the concrete hall of cellblock two with only their night vision cameras guiding the way. Snow and Cadence followed along with them, Roy Pruitt in tow. The living swung their cameras to and fro, peering into cells as if they expected to find some long-lost prisoner still alive in his cell, just waiting to be found. The residual spirits, mere recordings of the people they once were, moving in loops, went unseen as they paced their cells, slept on beds that long ago had the mattresses removed from the frames, or stood by the bars, waiting for something. All of them were unseen by the three breathers as they recorded.

"I thought there would be more spirits here," Cadence said, her voice quiet.

"Ain't like walls stop 'em anymore, missy," Roy said. "They move 'round the prison as they see fit now. Could be anywhere 'round here, really."

"As a monitor, I would have thought you would have a general idea of where they were," Snow said, his voice also quiet, though Cadence caught the hint of disapproval in his tone.

"Eh, they're prolly all in the cafeteria," Roy said with a dismissive shrug.

"Where the riot happened that killed you?" Cadence saw Roy stiffen as she said that. A very small part of her took pleasure in making him uncomfortable.

"Yes," he replied, his voice curt.

"Sorry," she said after Snow gave her a pointed look. *Do not taunt an unhappy, not-fun-ball monitor,* she thought to herself. She received the message loud and clear without Snow having to say a word.

"Let's set up the camera here," Liam said as they came to a stop mid-way down the corridor.

"Swivel one, right?" Teeny stopped and put down the backpack she had been carrying.

"You got it," Liam said as he looked around. It was dark, but they could make out the cells on the two floors in the dim light of their flashlights. "Seems too quiet."

"Maybe they are just drawing on energy, biding their time. It's early yet," Teeny said as Aiden helped her secure the camera onto the tripod they had rigged with a swivel.

"Still, this hardly seems worth all of the hand-wringing and doomsaying that Aiden and his friends were doing yesterday," Liam said.

"I can hear you," Aiden said with a glower toward Liam.

"I know," Liam said, dismissing whatever offense he might have given with his words. He didn't really care if he had offended Aiden or hurt his feelings. So far, this place had been a dud. Duds didn't make for good television.

"The most Dan and I got here were footsteps and the sound of cell doors closing," Aiden said, speaking to Teeny only as if Liam weren't there at all.

"Well, here's hoping—" Cadence began, but Snow cut her off.

"Don't you dare finish that sentence, young lady," Snow said, knowing exactly what she was going to say. "You'll only end up inviting more trouble down onto all of us."

"Come on! Are you guys sleeping or what?" Liam's yell echoed back, reverberating through the cell block. "Make a noise. Touch one of us. I thought you were big bad criminals. Are you too afraid of us to make a noise?"

"Dude, that's a bad idea," Aiden said, attempting to get Liam to stop taunting the spirits.

"Is that guy serious?" Roy asked, turning to Snow and Cadence.

"I would love to say no, but I think he is," Cadence said.

"If he gets the spirits left here riled up, they'll do more'n touch him." Roy frowned. "And then do worse to that little girl that's with him."

"I'll take care of it." Cadence sighed.

Before Snow could ask her what she meant, Cadence had teleported to the second floor. She disappeared into one and then came out, cradling something in her hands. She was using a little energy to carry whatever it was; Snow could tell that much. She flung her hands out, and pebbles and small stones rained down, clattering to the floor. One hit Liam on the shoulder, but none went near Teeny or Aiden unless they happened to bounce that way after hitting the floor. Cadence then rejoined Snow and Roy. The former looked more bemused than anything, while the latter looked unimpressed and a little annoyed.

"I guess someone wants you to pipe down," Teeny said with a laugh.

"One of those rocks hit me," Liam said, a slight whine in his voice.

"Well, you got what you asked for, man," Aiden said, trying hard not to laugh along with Teeny. He couldn't hide the slight smile, however.

"That should hopefully appease him," Snow said. "However, you needn't have hit him with one of the stones."

"I swear I didn't aim. I just tossed," Cade said. "One of them hitting him was pure, joyful luck." She gave Snow one of her practiced innocent smiles, and Snow knew there was zero innocence behind it.

"You, my dear, are incorrigible," Snow teased.

"And you wouldn't have it any other way." Cade smiled.

Snow tried to look disapproving, but Cade could see the smile he was trying to hide. The breathers, in the meantime, had finished setting up their camera, which was now rotating slowly as it recorded. Liam had pulled out his audio recorder and was getting ready to try to see if he could capture any ghostly voices or sounds.

"They just threw stones at you, dude. Are you sure you want to do that?" Aiden had his doubts about Liam's methods and the results they would get.

"Well, the stones are a good indication someone is here and wanting to communicate, even if they just want to tell me to shut up," Liam replied.

Aiden could understand why they would want to tell him to shut up. In fact, he was shocked that a small rain of stones was all they had gotten from Liam's shouting. Aiden also knew that any skeptic worth their salt would look at that footage and say it was possible that the echo reverberations had knocked some loose stones down, given the disrepair the building was in. All in all, he was certain either Snow or Cadence had done it to mess with Liam. And he really couldn't blame them.

Liam hit "record" on the handheld device and held it out as if he was trying to hand it to someone. "If any spirit in this prison wishes to communicate with us, please come over and talk into this machine in my hand. It will pick up your voice. Draw on our energy and talk to us." He was silent for a few moments before speaking up again. "Why did you throw stones at us?"

"Because you're a pain in my ass," Cadence muttered under her breath. At that moment, a cell door slammed on the second floor. Cadence looked over to Snow. "Okay, that one wasn't me."

"That was prolly Bison," Roy said with a shrug. "Now that he knows he's got himself an audience, he'll make a ruckus." As if to prove that point, another cell door banged, sounding like it had opened.

The breathers stayed quiet, their eyes straining. "I don't see anything opening or closing," Teeny said.

"Yeah, but we sure can hear it," Liam said.

Three more clangs sounded in succession, and Snow disappeared from his spot. Cadence saw him reappear upstairs. Another ghost appeared beside him in just the pants of his prison uniform. His brown hair was long and wild, hanging almost to his waist, and knotted like it hadn't been brushed in a long time. Cade could see Snow arguing with the man. The man that Roy had called Bison stormed back into a cell, slamming the cell door.

"I caught that one," Teeny said, excitement in her voice. "Upstairs, right up there." She pointed. "The cell door slammed shut hard enough to bounce back open!"

Snow rejoined Cadence and Roy. "That should take care of that," Snow said with a decisive nod.

Roy chuckled. "You don't know Bison."

Bison came back out of the cell holding something. He threw it, and for a moment, Cadence thought he was using her trick of just tossing pebbles.

Half of a cinder block sailed through the air from the second floor after Bison threw it. It landed and crashed into pieces inches from the camera, sending up a plume of dust and dirt. All three breathers held their breath for a moment, staring at the brick.

The breathers were all straining their ears, trying to catch any errant sound, but it was quiet. It seemed Bison was done throwing his fit, having gotten the reaction he was hoping for: stunned silence. It took a moment for the breathers to relax enough to remember that they were rolling audio recorders. After asking a couple more generic questions, Liam rolled the recording back as Teeny trained her video camera on him. As the audio played back, Liam was clearly heard, but his voice was the only one heard. Despite the noises caught of the cell doors slamming, the stones landing, and the cinder block crashing to the floor, there were no voices.

"Come on," Teeny said. "I think we've seen all this cell-block is going to do. Let's head to the cafeteria. Isn't that where the kid said the riot took place in the '70s?"

"The kid's name is Derrick," Aiden said, finding himself irritated by their continued use of the word kid when referring to Derrick. He knew he shouldn't be irked by it; he called Derrick "kid" all the time. He just wanted Derrick to get credit by name for all the research he did on this place, especially since they were talking about him on camera.

"Yeah, let's give it a try. Hopefully, it's got a little more to it than this cellblock," Liam said. He was being cavalier and pretending that the whole cinder block incident hadn't spooked him. He was also pointedly ignoring Aiden's irritation at calling Derrick a kid.

Leaving the swivel camera to record whatever activity it might be lucky enough to catch, the three breathers left for the prison's cafeteria. Roy teleported ahead to make sure the spirits there would behave. Snow and Cadence drifted along with the breathers, hoping that the rest of the night went this smoothly. The group retraced their steps down the long cellblock to the atrium and turned to make their way down the shorter hall.

"What's that?" Liam pointed to a doorway that was covered halfway with stones, boards, and debris.

"That would be the rec room where the *Ripley's* show guys were hurt," Aiden said.

"I wonder if we could dig the door out and get in there," Liam mused as he stopped to look at the door.

"Are you insane?" It was Teeny who replied. Aiden hadn't had the chance to even open his mouth. Teeny hit Liam on the arm for good measure. "I may not think this place is as dangerous as Aiden is worried it is, but I am not going to go in there. That's asking for trouble."

"Looks like both the young lady and Aiden have better heads on their shoulders than this Liam fellow," Snow noted.

"Thank God," Cadence agreed.

"Yeah," Roy added. "None of us go in there, an' I ain't so sure anyone alive would walk out in the same shape they went in."

"Come on." Aiden tried to usher the other two along. "The cafeteria's right here."

The swinging double doors of the cafeteria were still intact across the hall from the rec room. The cafeteria doors opened when Liam pushed on them, but their hinges squeaked, shrill and loud. Teeny and Aiden followed Liam in, with Snow and Cadence right behind them. The barred windows, most of them missing their glass, let a little bit of moonlight in when it peeked through the overhead clouds. Graffiti covered the long wall to the left; to the right, the metallic serving station, dented and rusty, was still bolted to the floor. Dust, dirt, and cobwebs were all over, and many of the ceiling tiles had fallen, exposing the ducts and disconnected wiring above.

Cadence and Snow could see Roy over in one corner with about ten inmates' spirits. So far, the inmates seemed content to just watch the breathers and see what they did, but there was an air of tension in the room that was underlined with a feeling of malice. Both Cadence and Snow felt it immediately and exchanged a worried look.

"Aiden, you and Dan were in here before, right?" Liam was looking a little on edge, sensing the same aggressive tension that the ghosts were aware of.

"Yeah, but we didn't stay too long," Aiden answered.

"Why?" Teeny inquired.

"Because it felt like this." Aiden was panning his handheld camera around the room as he answered.

"If there are any spirits in this room, can you make a noise for us? Maybe knock on the wall or swing the doors?" Teeny's voice echoed in the room with an unmistakable nervousness.

Roy made his way over to Cadence and Snow, and once he had done so, the spirits began to fan out around the room. They walked around the breathers, watching them like predators hunting prey. One of the inmates kicked the serving station, a metallic thump echoing out into the large room. The three breathers all turned toward the station, and Teeny began to advance toward it.

"Be careful," Aiden cautioned.

"We know what we're doing," Liam snapped at Aiden. He followed Teeny toward the old piece of cafeteria equipment.

"Thank you. Can you do it again? Give us two thumps, nice and loud, please," Teeny requested.

"That girl is gonna be trouble," Roy said in his southern accent. "She's eggin' 'em on."

Two more kicks were given from the serving station, this time louder. The inmate doing the kicking was grinning, having fun leading the woman toward him. There was nothing nice in his grin. Two other inmates were circling Liam, keeping pace with him as he moved toward Teeny. Another one hung back next to Aiden, while others were content to watch from various places in the room.

"Thank you," Teeny said in response to the kicks. "Can you do something else? Can you yell or whistle?"

The spirit that had been doing the kicking looked over at Roy. "She's cute an' all, but does she think we're some circus animals doin' tricks or some shit?"

Roy shrugged. "No idea what she thinks, Billy. You know what to do."

"Mr. Pruitt," Snow said, "I do hope that you are not up to something. As the location monitor—"

"Location monitor." Roy spat the words out of his mouth as if they were venomous. "Let me tell you just how much I love bein' stuck in this hellhole I was killed in, with half the bastards responsible for what led to my death. But don't you worry that pretty little head; I know my job." He then turned and made his way over to Billy at the serving station.

"I don't like where this is going." Cadence moved closer to Snow.

"Nor I," Snow affirmed. "But until a line is crossed, there is little we can do."

"And if he plans to cross that line tonight? Aiden, we were able to rationalize with. I don't think some Hollywood production company is going to be quite so willing to hide evidence," Cadence worried aloud. "Not to mention, with the bad things Whitfield said were here, how do we keep the living safe if he does decide to go bad?"

"Calm down," Snow soothed. "He could just be doing and saying half of this to get a rise out us. For now, just wait and see. But be ready, just in case."

CHAPTER 17

Bedtime

Ava stayed close by Lauren and Derrick as her parents picked up the pots and pans that had crashed to the floor when the ghost of Emma had dropped the mounted ceiling unit in the kitchen. Emma stared at Ava, fury in her eyes as she walked unseen past Ava's parents and toward the little girl.

"So much anger," Lauren said, her voice quiet as she reacted to the anger radiating off of the small spirit.

"Keep Ava between you and Derrick," Sam said to Lauren. He then moved to put himself in between Emma and Lauren.

"Why are you here?" Emma demanded.

"You're scaring the little girl and her family. That's why," Sam responded.

"You aren't wanted here," Emma said, her southern accent thick.

"Neither are you," Sam replied. He hated to be so blunt or mean to a child, spirit or breather, but there was no way he was going to let her harm anyone.

"This is my property." Emma stamped her foot for emphasis. "The people here belong to me. Daddy said so."

"Your father is here?" Sam couldn't believe her father would be letting her get away with this, if he was a ghost. But then, some parents weren't good at disciplining and not spoiling their children.

"Daddy's gone. So's Mama. Daddy said that when they were gone, all the land, and everyone on it, would be mine. So, you have no right to be here. My land, my people. Stop trying to interfere."

Sam shook his head and followed a hunch as he asked another question. "What was this land used for?"

"This side of the plantation was mostly housing," Emma said as she gave a shrug of her small shoulders. "The other side was where the slaves worked in the fields. Except for those worthy enough to work in the house, of course."

Emma was indeed the daughter of a plantation owner. It seemed to Sam that she had been brought up to believe she was better than everybody else, as would have been normal for the time and her station. Sam had known from Derrick's research that the family had long been in the area and had once been quite rich and influential, but he hadn't known why.

"Things aren't like that anymore," Sam said. "They haven't been for a long time now. You need to leave this family. They don't want you here, Emma."

"What do you know?" she argued, her face red with anger. She then disappeared from sight.

"Sorry," Robin said as she and Doug rejoined Lauren and Derrick.

"Why are you apologizing?" Lauren asked. "You didn't do that. You aren't responsible for what is going on here. None of you are. This is a spirit that's been attached to the land, and she got attached to your family, likely because she misses her own."

"It's my fault," Ava said, as tears fell from her eyes. "'Cause I saw her and talked to her. 'Cause I thought we were friends."

Robin and Doug knelt down in front of their daughter and pulled her into a hug in between them. "It's not your fault, honey," Doug said. "You had no way of knowing."

"No one blames you," Robin said, assuring her daughter. "This is not your fault."

Lauren and Derrick stepped back a little to let the family have their space. Derrick looked over his shoulder at the equipment still recording in the living room and was relieved to see it still intact. After what Emma had done to the camera when the three of them had been there to talk to Robin initially, he had been afraid that while their attention was on the kitchen and the family, the ghost would have done something to the setup. What he didn't see was that Sarah had been in the family room, guarding the things they had left behind when they went to investigate Emma's tantrum.

Sam saw Sarah and walked over to the pretty little African-American girl. "Why are you stuck with her?"

"I was her friend," Sarah said.

"Her friend or her slave?" Sam was dubious that the gentle girl in front of him was a genuine friend of the spoiled brat that Emma was.

"Does it matter?" Sarah looked down as she replied, her fingers fidgeting together.

"It matters to me," Sam said. "Slavery was abolished a long time ago. You don't belong to her anymore. You don't have to stay loyal to her because you think it is your place to."

Sarah looked up at Sam as the breathers filtered back into the family room to take up their positions for the investigation once more. She looked doubtful but also hopeful, torn between the two emotions.

"Sarah," a young female voice screeched. Emma appeared beside the startled ghost girl, grabbed her arm, and the two of them disappeared as Emma teleported them off some place.

Ava settled back down on the couch with her mother and Doug sat down in a recliner nearby. Lauren retook her spot on the sofa as Derrick began manning the camera again. Sam stayed near Lauren and couldn't help but notice Ava's eyes darting back and forth from Lauren to him.

"Who is he?" Ava asked. "You never told me."

"Who, baby?" Robin asked.

"The man, there," Ava said, her voice calm as she pointed in the general direction of Lauren, but off to one side. Derrick swung the camera to where she pointed, but he saw nothing there. He moved the camera back toward the couch and found Lauren looking quite serious.

"He is one of the good guys. He helps protect me," Lauren explained.

"From people like Emma?" the little girl asked.

"Yes, from people like Emma and worse," Lauren said.

Robin looked lost and confused. "What are you guys talking about?"

"I have a spirit guardian. He is kind of like a guardian angel. He helps keep me safe when I need protection from more dangerous spirits." Lauren glanced over at Derrick and then back to Robin and Ava.

"Ava, did Emma give you anything to keep her tied to this house? Or did she say there was something here that she was attached to?" Lauren wondered if there was some kind of tether keeping the girl's spirit here. The land her family had owned had once comprised almost the whole county. While she knew that the parcel of land that Emma's family's home had been on had since been developed into this entire neighborhood, she had no idea why Emma had honed in on this house, this family.

"No," Ava said, shaking her head.

"Are there other children on this block?" Lauren asked, moving her gaze from the child to her parents.

"Next door, the Lewises have twins about a year older than Ava. Across the street is a little girl Ava's age. Two doors down on the left, they have three kids, twelve, ten, and eight," Robin answered.

"Plenty of kids around here," Doug said. "It's a very family-centric neighborhood. That's one reason we chose it."

Lauren nodded, thinking. With the choice of children around, there had to be a reason Emma stayed locked into this house, this family. Was it simply because Ava was an untrained medium, or could there be something else holding Emma here?

"Well, one thing you need to know is that Ava has the same ability I do," Lauren said, being careful to keep her voice calm, as she didn't want to alarm Robin or Doug. "Her gift might be stronger than mine, in fact. She is going to need help to learn how to protect herself from spirits, and I will be happy to help if you want me to. It's a gift, but it can be quite a double-edged sword."

"Are they going to come after her, like this one did?" Robin asked, concern for her daughter covering her face.

"To be fair, this one initially didn't come after her. It sounds like Emma approached Ava as a friend at first. It was only when Emma couldn't get her way that she started throwing temper tantrums. I think Emma was just not brought up with discipline. She was the spoiled daughter of a rich family, and she just doesn't fathom not getting her way."

"But with all the kids and families here, is that why she latched on to Ava?" Doug asked.

"It's possible," Lauren said with a nod. "I would say at this point that it is either that or there is something in, under, or around this house that ties her here. A favorite toy, her bones, I don't know."

"So, how do we proceed? It's not like we can just move," Doug said.

"No, and you shouldn't have to," Lauren agreed. She turned to Derrick and said, "You can stop the recording for now."

Ava yawned, and Robin hugged her. "I think it's time to start getting you ready for bed, sweetheart."

"I'm not sleepy," Ava said, uttering the usual protest of bedtime given by sleepy children.

"Sure, sure," Doug said with a chuckle. "Go on up with Mom for your bath, okay, kiddo? I'll be up in a bit to say goodnight."

Robin got up and took Ava's hand, leading her out of the room and up the stairs. Lauren waited until she heard the water running upstairs before beginning to outline her plan with Derrick and Doug.

"Doug, could we set up a camera or two in Ava's room? I would like to monitor that room while she tries to sleep."

"Sure," Doug said with a nod.

"Thanks," Lauren said. "Derrick, can you set up the cameras and have a live feed going to your laptop? Set yourself up at the kitchen table. Then I want you to dig a little more into the family history of Emma. See what details you can find on this tragedy that befell her family."

"On it." Derrick nodded. He grabbed one of the large plastic cases he had hauled in and went upstairs. Derrick was enjoying the fact that he was getting to play Aiden's part tonight and be the tech guy. He had been learning so much from Aiden that he was glad he had a chance to display all he had learned.

"I would suggest putting Ava to bed as normal and watching. I have a feeling that, as riled up as Emma is, she isn't going to let Ava fall asleep," Lauren said.

"Do you think Emma will try to hurt her?" Doug leaned forward in his chair, worried.

"I doubt it. Emma seems to see you and Robin more as her enemies, not Ava. I think she will likely try to talk to her. But we will be watching over her just to make sure," Lauren said, giving Doug a comforting smile.

CHAPTER 18

Heads Up!

The animosity and anger in the cafeteria of the dilapidated prison was palpable, even to the breathers. They moved at a snail's pace, every motion deliberate, as if they were walking through a swamp, trying not to disturb alligators. The investigators' cameras were rolling, and their other handheld instruments were all going as they swept them from side to side.

"Mr. Pruitt," Snow said. "I suggest you rein in your charges. They look as if they are about to attack the investigators."

"So, what if they do?" Roy argued as he turned to the side and spat once again. "Stupid breathers pokin' their noses where they don't belong. Who's to mind if they get a little banged up?"

"Well, for one, we mind," Snow stated, his voice and tone calm but firm. Cadence knew his body language better, however. He was standing straight with his hands loose at his sides. He was ready to act if need be.

"I'm pretty sure they'd mind, too," Cadence added.

"Damn, you two are easy," Roy said after a moment, breaking into a large smile. Some of the inmates snickered. "Almost ain't worth tryin' to get yer goat."

One of the inmates near Liam reached over and tugged on the bottom of the ghost hunter's coat hard enough to pull him back a step.

"Woah, did you see that?" Liam exclaimed. His excitement elicited a round of quiet laughter from the inmates.

The inmate who pulled the jacket looked over at Snow and Cadence. "Gotta give them a little something to talk about, right?" the man said. There was still an edge to the man's voice and an underlying threat in the atmosphere that hadn't eased, despite Roy trying to pass all this off as a joke.

"See what?" It was Teeny who turned to talk to Liam.

"Something tugged the back of my coat hard enough to pull me back," Liam said. "Damn, were you not watching?"

"I was facing that way, sorry," she said as she gestured to the wall that held the door back out to the hall and cellblocks.

A couple of the inmates wandered back into the kitchen area behind the food service counter. Another round of snickers went up from the six other spirits left in the room with the breathers, including Roy. Snow frowned, and Cadence limped over toward the kitchen to see what the other two were up to. Part of Snow wanted to argue, not wanting to leave Cadence alone with any of the inmates with the shape she was in. He also knew that if he said anything, she would be less than appreciative of his concern.

"I wasn't looking, but my camera was pointed toward you. It might have caught something." Aiden moved forward from the back of the room. Both Snow and Cadence moved over to the group of the living as they huddled around the camera Aiden held as he rewound the last few minutes of footage.

"There!" Liam crowed, his voice echoing in the empty concrete room. "You can see the pull on my coat."

Aiden rewound the footage once more, and sure enough, the fact that Liam's coat was tugged on was clear. There was nothing visible that could have tugged on it, and nothing around Liam it could have snagged on.

Snow nodded a bit. This was exactly the kind of thing that the ghosts were allowed to do. No other evidence was there, just the inexplicable tug—no figures or phantom hands on the coat. He relaxed a little. Mr. Pruitt did seem to have this all well in hand, after all.

"We know what we're doin' around here," Roy said. "And these guys, most of 'em that's left here anyway, they ain't so bad. Just had nuthin' ta do fer too long, is all."

"Just bored," the inmate who tugged on Liam's coat said as he reached up to scratch at his chin beneath his brown beard. "Messing with these guys is about the only fun we get to have anymore." With that, he flicked Liam in the ear before stepping away and walking out the door of the cafeteria.

"Ow!" Liam jumped, his head tilting to one side as he quickly covered his ear.

"Now what?" Teeny's voice expressed both her exasperation with her partner's antics and excitement about the possible activity as Liam jumped and covered his ear.

"Someone pinched my ear," he said, his tone somewhat petulant.

"Isn't touching you exactly what you asked them to do?" Aiden couldn't believe the guy was such a baby about such a small thing.

Cadence snickered as she returned from the kitchen, hearing Liam complain. Snow gave her a somewhat disapproving look, though he was fighting to hide his own smile as well. Cadence rejoined Snow with a shrug. "They left the kitchen."

"Yeah, I was fine with the tug on my coat, thank you," Liam said, his voice sharp as he replied to Aiden. "Big difference between a touch and a touch that hurts."

"Okay, so, then you only want the ghosts to give you good touches, not bad touches?" Teeny said, a smile crooking the corner of one side of her mouth. "Should we teach them the 'No-No Square' song?"

"Very funny," Liam said with a huff. "Let's just keep moving."

"Um, no," Teeny said. "This is where that riot took place in the '70s. A bunch of people were killed. We should stay and try some communicating."

"They're communicating," Liam said. "They have touched and pinched. I thought you wanted to set up your experiment."

"I do, but we have time," Teeny said. She sat down on the dirty, dusty floor, crossing her legs. "Right now, I think we need to do a little work in here. Aiden, we usually sit back to back so that our body cameras are facing out; that way we have a better chance of recording anything that happens. So, let's all sit back to back in a kind of triangle and do some EVP."

Aiden nodded and took a seat on the floor next to her, turned slightly. Liam joined them, and they sat on the cold floor, feeling the iciness of the winter weather seep up into their flesh from the concrete. They were shoulder-to-shoulder, their body cameras and handheld cameras catching most of the room.

"For all their sniping with each other and prissiness, they're smart on their coverage," Cadence said.

"Yes, but most of the spirits have left the cafeteria at this point. Which is probably good since Liam there has proven he is easy to unsettle," Snow said.

"No kidding. Hell, I half want to go mess with Liam just to see his reaction," Cadence said with a mischievous grin.

"Cadence," Snow said, his tone one of warning.

"Oh, calm down, Ozzie. I'm not going to do it. But the temptation is strong to do it just to piss him off." She grinned again, and despite Snow shaking his head she knew he was amused, at the very least. "You have to admit it's funny. He acts all tough, calling out the ghosts, insulting them. But then when something happens to him, he gets all upset and pouty about it."

"We want to contact the spirits of those killed in the prison riot forty years ago," Teeny said, holding out her voice recorder. "Are you here with us?"

Roy wandered back over to Snow and Cadence after the last inmate left the cafeteria. "They've gone back to their cells. Night ain't a good time to be wanderin' around this place." He turned and looked over at the three breathers sitting on the floor and shook his head. "Dumb as the dirt they're sittin' on, ain't they?"

"Why do you say that, Mr. Pruitt?" Snow's clipped British accent made every utterance sound prim and proper, even if what he said was just conversational.

"Well," Roy said. "Number one they're sitting on a bare concrete floor in what is now pretty much an open room to the outdoors since the glass has been broken out of the windows, and it's winter. They're gonna catch their death if they stay there too long. And B, 'cause they're here at night. I'm tellin' ya, this ain't a place to mess with at night."

Cadence decided to ignore the mixed bullet point references. "You keep saying that, and I know you and Whitfield were talking about some kind of thing made from bits of souls killed here, but what makes it so dangerous? Does it kill breathers? Ghosts? Hurt people?"

"It just is." Roy shrugged. "You see the broken glass over there, that window?" He pointed out the broken window closest to the archway that led back into the kitchen.

"Yeah," Cadence said.

"About five years ago, it chased a couple of teenagers that had snuck in here one summer night. Guess they thought this would be a good place to canoodle or something. It picked the boy up and threw the kid into the window. That's what busted it out. The little Romeo was all cut up. Ended their sexy time pretty quick."

"I thought those things didn't leave the rooms they were in. The rec room and the gallows building outside," Cadence questioned.

"They usually don't," Roy said with a shrug. "I ain't sure what the hell it thought it was doin'. Maybe the little lovers' presence drew it out. But once we knew it was wanderin', we stayed well the hell out of its way."

"You didn't try to protect the teens?" Cadence was having a tough time trying to figure out how this guy got to be the monitor of the prison when he so obviously had little interest in doing his actual job.

"We protect ourselves," Roy said. "The livin' wanna be idiots and come creeping around in here, that's on them."

"Where were our predecessors, then?" Snow asked. "Surely, if breathers were present, they needed to be as well."

"Your predecessors didn't come round this way too often. I'd call, and they'd say they were in the middle of something more important. Dunno if that was the truth or if they just didn't feel like comin' out," Roy said with a shrug. "As for the thing," he said as he turned to address Cadence's question, "it was the one from the rec room. We'd started tryin' to barricade that place, but the couple, I guess, thought that the rec room would be a good place to try first. They went in there, but the lil' chickadee got spooked. So they came in here. It followed 'em. That's when we started workin' to make the barricade a lil' more difficult for the breathers to get by."

"Is there anything you can do about this creature?" Cadence asked.

"While I appreciate your faith in my abilities, missy, I ain't no match for that thing. Ain't seen it kill none of us, but I know it can hurt us. Given you're already hurt, you might wanna keep well out of its way," Roy said. He gestured to her legs, indicating he had seen her limping earlier.

"I'm fine," Cadence reassured him.

"Fine or not, I think, in this instance, it is best to follow Mr. Pruitt's advice," Snow said.

"Leroy Pruitt," Aiden called out, and all three ghosts in the room turned their attention toward him. "I know you were a guard here at the prison and that you were killed during the riot forty years ago. If you are here with us now, if you can hear me, give us a sign. We just want to talk to you."

Roy spat and shook his head. "Damned breathers," he muttered. "These so-called investigators come in here and rile things up, think they have the answers, act all high and mighty. You know what they want, though?"

"Evidence of life after death," Cadence said matter-of-factly.

"No. They want a fuckin' dog doin' tricks. Pardon my language, missy," he said as an afterthought. "They come traipsing through here with their cameras and all these other high-tech doodads. All it ever boils down to, though, is them askin' us to do tricks for them like we're puppies they're training. Speak up, bang on something, touch 'em, whistle, throw something. I musta missed the part in dyin' when I signed up to perform in some crazy ass three-ring circus." Roy shook his head in disgust and walked out of the cafeteria.

"Well, I guess we figured out what's bothering him," Cadence said to Snow as they both turned and looked back over at the three ghost hunters who were trying to get a recording of a ghostly voice on tape. The breathers were unaware only two ghosts were left in the room, and neither one was going to give them any audio to use.

CHAPTER 19

Lights Out

Derrick was situated at the end of the kitchen table, his laptop plugged into the wall behind him. Cords were running from upstairs to his computer, and he went back and forth between the video feed from Ava's bedroom and the tabs in his web browser that he was using for research. Lauren had settled in beside him and was meditating, trying to center herself. Sam was by her side, helping reinforce the protections she had placed.

Robin and Doug were still upstairs, putting Ava to bed. The little girl was restless and upset by the evening's events, which was understandable given all that had gone on. They sat on either side of her canopy bed, holding her hands. Each parent had a Dr. Seuss book in hand. Doug was reading to her as Robin waited. The nonsensical words seemed so innocent to Derrick, who remembered the story. He felt terrible for the family having to face this angry spirit.

It took about half an hour for the parents to get their daughter settled in her bed enough for them to go. The night light was left on, and the door was left open a crack so that the light from the hall could illuminate the room a little. Robin and Doug finally made their way back to the kitchen.

"Does anyone want some coffee? I have a feeling it might be a long night." Robin moved to the coffeemaker on the counter.

"I'll take you up on that," Derrick said, and her husband echoed the sentiment.

Lauren took a deep breath and opened her eyes. "Is she settled?" she asked Doug.

"Yeah. Not sure if she will stay in bed," he added. "But she is all tucked in for now."

"How is the research going, Derrick?" Lauren turned her gaze to her compatriot.

"Okay," he said. "Being in college gives you the advantage of access to thousands of online archives and libraries you might not otherwise have access to. It seems someone did a whole paper on this tragedy for a class."

"History class?" Lauren was surprised, as she couldn't imagine a history class accepting an assignment on local history. College classes tended to have a broader spectrum. At least, in her day, they did.

"No..." Derrick trailed off as he scrolled back up. "Um, Abnormal Psych, actually."

Lauren's eyebrows shot up at that. "Really? That's weird."

"How exactly does the history of the land fall into the category of abnormal psychology?" Doug shifted a bit in his chair as the smell of coffee began wafting through the kitchen.

"Okay, bear with me because this is going to be a story," Derrick said. "Also, I preface this with the fact that this is someone else's report, not mine and not my own research. Give me more time, and I can probably corroborate or debunk it, but since we are under the gun, I'll run with what I pulled in the search.

"We all know the Bartons had a lot of land; almost the whole county was theirs. Some had been developed into a plantation, slave quarters, empty fields so they could rotate where they grew crops each season, and some land left alone. Barton had five kids, but only one of them, the eldest, was a son. When the son got married, Old-Man Barton carved out a good-sized chunk of land for him and his wife to have as their own.

"Time went on, and a couple of years into the marriage, after a miscarriage, the young Barton couple had a child, a daughter. This would be Emma. This was back in the 1850s; slavery was a hotly contested issue, but we're below the Mason-Dixon Line, so you know how that went before the war. So, the young Barton family had slaves just the same as the older Barton had at the main estate a couple of miles from here.

"When Emma was seven years old, there was a fire at her home that killed her, her parents, their newborn son, and a couple of house slaves. I think we're safe to assume one of the house slaves killed was Sarah. Here is where we start to stray from history and into the story. Accounts from family members and the family members of former slaves, things like that."

Derrick paused and took a sip of the coffee that Robin had placed before him, and he grimaced as he realized, too late, that he hadn't added any cream or sugar to the drink. He corrected that, as Robin had put both of those things on the table and took another sip. He then continued with what he had found out.

"Okay, according to reports, Emma was kind of an odd duck. When she was four, one of her aunts found her in the yard of the home estate during a family event torturing a cat. The given excuse was that it scratched her, so she was punishing it, but whatever it was she did to the cat was extreme enough to make the aunt ill on the spot and rumor has it that Emma wasn't allowed to be without a chaperone much after that.

"That might be when Sarah entered the picture. It's said that Mrs. Barton's cook had a daughter around the same age as Emma and that the girls were friends. For that day and age, I think 'friend' was a way of putting it in polite terms.

"Anyway, there are stories that, despite Sarah's presence with her, Emma still took delight in torturing animals. For years, the family tried to pass it off as a phase and even blamed Sarah for letting Emma get away with doing those kinds of things. Then Emma, at six, according to reports, took her delight in others' pain to a new level.

"There was a slave who had taken ill. Some say they were a relative of Sarah's, other stories say they were just a different slave on the estate. Either way, both accounts agree that Emma somehow lost Sarah that day and went to where the slave was. She killed him, but that was after she hurt him. He was too old and weak from illness to really fight her off, and given she was white, he probably wouldn't have, anyway."

"Jesus," Doug murmured.

"Yeah, this kid was psycho in life. Another story has it that one night the family was awakened by this terrible screaming coming from the stable. Emma was found there skinning an animal strip by strip while it was still alive. The stories say that was when Old-Man Barton told his son and daughter-in-law that enough was enough.

"They planned to send Emma to a boarding school in the hopes that it might have a better effect on the child. The couple argued about it, as Mrs. Barton didn't want to send her only child away. That changed when Mrs. Barton discovered she was pregnant. No one in the family wanted to have a defenseless infant around Emma, so the decision was made for a European boarding school. Emma was less than thrilled with the decision.

"She got up in the middle of the night and managed to barricade her parents in their room after starting a fire in their bed. The season had been dry, so the house went up like tinder in a box. The fire spread so fast that no one in the house made it out. Somehow, Emma's own sociopathy led to her death. Old-Man Barton was heartbroken over the loss of his only son and the lost continuation of his family line through his grandson. He had the remains of the homestead torn down, absorbed the livestock and slaves back into his own estate, and swore never to build there again. In fact, when he gave parcels of land to his daughters upon their marriages, they were all on the opposite side of the estate. This neighborhood development is the first thing that this land has been used for since."

"Dear God," Robin said softly before moving her hands to cover her mouth.

"That's awful," Doug said, slipping an arm around his wife.

"What does she want with our Ava?" Robin's haunted eyes turned to Lauren for answers as she asked the question.

Derrick clicked his mouse on the screen and went from the wall of text that had been the research paper to the video feed of Ava's room. The girl seemed to be asleep and was curled up on her side.

"From what I've seen," Lauren said, her words thoughtful, "I think she began here genuinely looking for a friend. Sarah is a possession to her; she doesn't think of the child as a friend or even as a person. At least, that's how it seems. But as you make rules and Ava follows them, especially ones that Emma, for whatever reason, doesn't like, she seems to be getting angrier and angrier. Today, that ended up with the attack on you. What we need to try to do is convince both Emma and Sarah to move on. I doubt Sarah will take much convincing; she seems reluctant to be here anyway, except to try to take the brunt of Emma's anger. Emma is going to be more difficult."

Robin sighed and shook her head. "I just don't know what to do anymore." Her hands were wrapped tightly around her mug. She had opted for hot tea instead of coffee, and she idly played with the paper tag of the tea bag with one finger as she stared into the drink's depths.

Doug reached over and caressed his wife's back. "It'll be okay. These guys are here to help us." He looked over at Lauren and Derrick and asked, "So, how did you guys get into doing this kind of thing, anyway?"

Lauren smiled. "I've always been able to see and communicate with spirits. When I was a child, perhaps Ava's age, just like her, I could see and talk to them like they were as solid as you and me. My mother thought I was crazy and told me to cut it out. She was more worried about the neighbors and what they thought of us than acting in support of my abilities. I think her being raised Catholic played into that a good bit as well.

"I stopped talking about it, and as I grew up, I figured out ways to shield myself, to control it a little. I denied it for a long time, ignored what I saw, and refused to communicate. I think I let my mother's fears overtake me a little. When I met my ex-husband, he had such a passionate interest in the supernatural; it kind of spurred me to admit what I could do. This was long before the rise of ghost-hunting shows on TV, but he liked to go investigate, and he accepted what I could do. Dan didn't think I was crazy." Lauren stopped and let her gaze fall to the table.

Derrick jumped into the conversation to allow Lauren time to recover. She had gotten much better now that she had been dealing with her grief in the last couple of months, but he didn't want to make this moment of sadness awkward. "I got lucky enough to fall in with these guys a couple of years ago," he said.

"How did you manage that?" Doug asked, still rubbing his wife's back as they talked.

"A girl I was dating at the time was into the whole New Age thing. She loved going to Lauren's shop. So around Christmas time, I went in there on my own to get her a gift and realized I had no idea what I was looking for. Aiden, our tech guy that Robin met the other day, was in the back area with Dan, and they were reviewing some footage they had taken on an investigation in a cemetery. I saw it over Aiden's shoulder and was instantly obsessed. I had to find out everything."

Lauren laughed. "I remember that. You came in the next day with a full report on the graveyard, its history, and the history of those buried there. I don't recall what you got your girlfriend, however."

Derrick gave a sheepish grin. "I forgot about a date when I was doing all that research that night. She wasn't really forgiving when it came to being stood up. She dumped me." The married couple laughed, the tension in the room abating as conversation flowed.

"Well, I have to apologize for my part in the whole crackpot thing," Doug said, looking at Lauren. "I was a bit like your mom when Robin proposed this whole thing to me. She was more willing to believe the truth of what was really going on than I was, and I have to admit I was worried what the neighbors would say if they found out."

Lauren nodded. "It's okay, Doug. Really. We tend to want to rationalize things. The people who don't rationalize seem to see ghosts everywhere, even if it is just bad plumbing, a settling house, or raccoons in their attic." This made everyone laugh again.

"I wish it were raccoons," Robin said. Although she was tired and annoyed at the situation, she had become far less jumpy as the conversation turned toward more normal things like old girlfriends and obsessive interests.

"How did you hear about us, anyway?" Lauren asked. "It's not like we advertise."

"Oh! My friend Amber is married to Michael Woods," Robin said. "She said you helped them put his mother's spirit to rest a couple of months ago when the people who bought the house were having issues."

"Wow," Derrick exclaimed. "Talk about a small world."

"No kidding," Lauren said.

Derrick glanced back down at the monitor, and the smile vanished from his face. "She's awake."

Sam glanced at the monitor and frowned; he could see the ghost child on the video feed. Her body language was aggressive. He had no choice. He had to let Cadence know what was going on and that he was alone. Whitfield still hadn't shown up.

Ava was sitting up on the edge of her bed and looked like she was talking to someone. Without warning, one hand raised as if it were being pulled on and it was plain that Ava was becoming more agitated by the second.

Derrick looked over to Lauren and nodded. "Get up there," he said. She was ahead of him and already out of her chair. Robin and Doug rose as well to go up to their daughter.

Then the lights went out.

CHAPTER 20

What Happens in Solitary

The footsteps of the three breathers echoed along the cold concrete hall of the prison as they made their way down to the block that comprised death row and solitary confinement. The night vision cameras showed their breath in the cold air as they walked without conversation. The change in atmosphere as they crossed the threshold into the cellblock was palpable and instantaneous. There was an anger, a depression, and a desperation that was easy to feel.

"Dear God." Teeny stopped in her tracks not far over the threshold.

"Yeah, this would be why Dan and I didn't venture too far in," Aiden agreed. "This is what I meant when I said that it just felt bad."

"Oh, come on," Liam complained, annoyance plain in his voice. "You two are psyching each other out. This is an abandoned prison in winter; it is going to have some obvious overtones that will have a psychological impact on how we react. Teeny, you know this well."

Teeny sighed and nodded, steeling herself against the onslaught of warning bells going off in her head. "You're right," she said. "We keep going to get to the truth."

"There you go." Liam nodded with approval. "Now, which do you want, a death row cell or a solitary confinement cell?"

"What?" Aiden wasn't sure what Liam was driving at.

"We do vigils in what are thought to be the most haunted areas of a place," Liam explained. "Given what you said about feeling like the place is bad, and what Derrick told us about the history of these areas, I want one of you in a death row cell and one of you in a solitary confinement cell. See what kind of evidence you can get."

"What about you?" Aiden asked.

"I stay out here in the hallway to help either of you in case there's trouble."

"Have you had something happen where someone needed help?" Aiden had never really watched their show. He couldn't sit through the theatrics of it.

"A couple of times doors have locked on their own," Teeny said.

"So, we always have someone nearby, not on a vigil, just to be sure nothing bad happens to the other one," Liam said, finishing the explanation.

Aiden sighed. He didn't really fancy being locked up in either kind of cell. He knew Snow and Cadence were here, or at least one of them was. He wasn't entirely sure how they would have worked things out with Lauren and Derrick off on the Owens case, but he knew they would never leave this place unattended, especially with a television show traipsing through the prison.

"I'll take solitary," Teeny volunteered in the quiet as Aiden was thinking.

"Solves that, then," Liam said. "Aiden, you get a death row cell."

"Snow, we have a problem," Cadence said as she looked at her phone, which had buzzed to alert her to a message.

"What a refreshing change," he said dryly. It was not lost on Cadence that he was using one of her phrases.

"Whitfield never showed up to watch over what was happening at the Owens' house. Sam is on his own."

"I know you are protective of your brother, Cadence, but I think he can handle a child on his own," Snow said as they both followed Liam and Aiden to the death row cells. Teeny had already put herself into a solitary cell.

"Oh, I don't doubt that. Sam said it was getting hairy over there, but he could handle it, but he did mention that Whitfield never showed," Cadence emphasized.

"Whitfield did say that he had some work on an NHD project that they wanted him to finish up first. Perhaps it's just taking longer than expected. We should bring it up to Alistair, however. He did make a point of saying that Whitfield is with us and can take on NHD projects only when we don't need him," Snow agreed.

The death row end of the cellblock was darker than the solitary end. The shadows seemed thicker here, almost as if they were physical things, not just the mere absence of light. It also seemed colder, even Liam was noticing it more. His voice still held steady, but as he reached out to open the cell door for Aiden, Aiden could see the man's hand shaking a little. Without commenting on it, Aiden stepped into the cell and sat himself down on the cold concrete floor. He put the handheld a little away from him, facing toward him, and in his hand was the audio recorder.

"You stay with him whilst I make sure the young lady stays safe?" Snow suggested.

"Sounds like a good idea," Cadence said with a nod. In the back of her mind, she was still worried about Sam. If what was happening at the house was bothering him enough to make him text her, it was serious. But on the other hand, she knew that she and Snow had to stay here. This investigation was in a more public forum, so it was more important that they keep the spirits here in line. That was their job. She just hoped the little brat that Sam was dealing with settled down.

Cadence limped into the cell and sat down next to Aiden, happy to be off her feet for a few minutes. There was something in the corner of the room, a kind of moving, undulating shadow that she didn't like. Across the walkway was the spirit of a condemned man, quite literally hanging in his cell, noose around his neck. His eyes were open, and he was leering at her and Aiden in a way that made her skin crawl.

Snow slipped into the room that Teeny had taken and was glad that he had opted to make sure she was safe. She wasn't alone, although she had no idea she wasn't. A ghost of a man in the blue uniform of the prison was sitting on the floor in the corner of the room, rocking back and forth, muttering incoherently.

Liam walked to the point that was mid-way between both Aiden and Teeny. He had company, as well. Roy was with him. He kept an eye on the television personality while he talked quietly with the residents who still occupied this wing of the prison.

In death row, Cadence brushed Aiden's hand to let him know she was there. He jumped slightly, then realized who it was, having caught a brief flash of her in his mind at the touch. He knew the cameras had recorded the jump, so he shook off his hand with a chuckle.

"Damn spider nearly scared me half to death."

Cade smiled, glad he had covered. She hadn't thought about the possibility of him reacting to her touch; she just knew she wanted him aware that he had backup. In the meantime, she was keeping a sharp eye on the shadow in the corner. *Was this one of the creatures that Whitfield had spoken of? Made up of the desperation of so many criminals facing their last days, bits of their souls that soured over time and never moved on?* Cadence wasn't sure, but she was uncomfortably aware of the fact that it looked a great deal like the chaos creature they had fought at Lexington Hills. Cadence stood and positioned herself between Aiden and the undulating shadows.

"Is there anyone here, in these cells on death row, that would like to communicate?" Aiden had the audio recorder running as he sat there, trying to catch an EVP.

A whine came from the shadowy thing in the corner, but it was nothing like the train-like cacophony of the chaos creature. Cadence relaxed her stance only a little, however. She had no idea if the creature could see her or even understand, but she shook her head at it, trying to indicate that it should stay quiet.

"We're not here to judge you," Aiden said. "We would like to help if we can. The device in my hand is something you can communicate through. Take energy from me if you need it and use it to talk to me."

Aiden felt ridiculous. He knew how things worked in the afterlife, to a greater degree than most of the living. He knew that Cadence would be there trying to keep the spirits from speaking too much, from giving away anything that would be concrete evidence of the world beyond the veil. Hell, he usually wasn't even the one who would be doing this. It would be Lauren and Derrick. He was just the tech guy, not the investigator. But here he was, making a fool of himself for the camera.

The shadow in the corner of the room moved as if it were taking a tentative step forward. Cadence moved a step as well, putting herself directly between it and Aiden. Another noise came from the creature, an echo that to Cadence sounded like many voices, but each voice could only make one certain sound. It was like a recitation of a poem except that there were many performers and each performer only got to say one letter of a word, and they were all trying to speak at the same time, out of order.

"Quiet," Cadence said, her voice a soft hiss.

Aiden shifted a bit, turning to look behind him. "I could swear I just heard something," he said. "I don't know what, though..." He narrowed his eyes, trying to peer into the lightless corner. He got to his feet and grabbed the handheld camera, aiming it at the corner where he thought the noise had come from. Aiming it at where the shadowy creature roiled in place, though the dancing shadows didn't show up on film. It was just a corner that looked a little dimmer in the night vision.

The shadows made another strange sound, almost like an electric hum, and the thing flew up to the ceiling to spread across the smooth surface like smoke. This movement did register on the camera as a few orbs moving up to the ceiling and then scattering in different directions.

Cadence looked up, watching it as it moved. She wasn't sure if she should be more on guard with it moving around or less, since it seemed to be ignoring them for the most part. She turned so that she was facing Aiden, as the shadows hung menacingly above them.

"Some orbs in that corner. Maybe something is trying to come through," Aiden half muttered to himself. He reached out with the hand that held the audio recorder, holding it out to the corner in question. "Who are you?"

The shadows on the ceiling began coalescing, swirling in a circle like clouds caught in a wind that signaled the start of a tornado. The man hanging from the rope in the cell across from them began laughing, the sound raspy and broken. Cadence turned and he had moved from his rope to the door of his cell. His neck was at an obscene angle as he watched. He pointed at Cadence and Aiden and just laughed.

That was when a muffled scream echoed from down the hall where Teeny had been closed into the solitary confinement cell. Liam ran, the jeers of the ghosts in the cells on either side of him going unheard. He skidded to a halt in front of the closed door of the solitary confinement cell Teeny had gone into. She was still screaming.

Although she hated leaving Aiden with the swirling shadows, Cadence ran through wall after wall, cell after cell, until she got into the one that Teeny was in. The old, dead prisoner that had been yammering nonsensically to himself when Teeny had gone into the cell had taken notice of her presence. She was sitting on the floor of the cell, her knees drawn up to her chest, eyes tightly closed, with her hands covering her ears as she screamed. The crazy spirit had managed to move to her and wrap his arms around her. His insane, nonsensical monologues hadn't stopped, but instead of muttering them to himself, he was now screaming them into Teeny's ear as he held her close. The joints in his hands were swollen, forcing them into a crooked, claw-like form. His long hair brushed Teeny's arms. Liam swung the door open as Cadence tried prying the crazy inmate off of Teeny, wondering where Snow was.

"TOO MANY SHADOWS! THE SHADOWS WILL EAT YOU! ALL YOU WILL BE IS SHADOW! THEY WON'T LET YOU LEAVE, LIKE THEY WON'T LET ME LEAVE! EVERYONE ELSE GETS TO GO, BUT NOT YOU, AND NOT ME! WE'RE IN HERE FOR GOOD! THEY'LL DRAG YOU OUT FEET FIRST BECAUSE THE SHADOWS ARE GOING TO EAT YOU! PRETTY LITTLE MORSEL FOR THE SHADOWS!" The inmate was screaming, his foul smell surrounding the small, trembling woman.

"Get off of her," Cadence hissed as she grabbed one of the old man's arms.

"Teeny!" Liam shouted, rushing in to help her. She flinched as he grabbed her hand, afraid that it was another spirit coming to take her. "Teeny, it's me. It's Liam."

"Come on, let the nice breather go," Cadence coaxed while tugging hard on his arm. She managed to pull one arm off of Teeny, which upset the balance of both, and they tumbled to their sides. Cadence took advantage of the situation and dragged the insane inmate back over to the corner she had initially seen him in.

"What on earth happened?" Snow asked, coming back into the room, which drew a glare from Cadence.

"Where were you? I thought you were here watching over her?" Cade said, her voice sharp.

"I was," Snow said. "Mr. Pruitt told me that Liam looked to be in more danger, so he asked to trade stations. I went out to him, and Mr. Pruitt came in here. Was he in here?"

"Nope," Cade said with a shake of her head. "I ran in when I heard the screaming and found this guy wrapped around her like a boa constrictor, yelling his crazy crap into her ear. Why do I feel like Roy is the male version of Carmen Sandiego?"

"Carmen Sandiego," Snow said, repeating the name. "Who is that?"

Cadence arched an eyebrow at Snow and then shook her head. "You've never heard of the books, or show, or games about Carmen Sandiego? It was a thing when I was a kid. *Where in the World is Carmen Sandiego?* You had to try to figure out where she was. It taught geography to kids without them really knowing it."

"And how is that like Mr. Pruitt?"

"Because we always seem to be asking where in the world he is," Cade replied, her tone dry.

Liam was crouched on the ground beside Teeny, trying to comfort her. "Shhhh, I've got you. It's okay. It's okay."

"Liam … Oh God, Liam, it was awful," Teeny said, tears still rolling down her face.

"You want to talk about it?" Liam stroked her hair, still trying to comfort her.

"Get me out of this cell first," Teeny replied.

The clanking of metal signified one of the cell doors being shaken and everyone paused, hearing a male voice echoing down the hallway.

"Shit, Aiden," Cadence said and teleported back to the cell he was in.

Liam helped Teeny up, and they went back down the hallway to where Aiden was shaking the door of his cell.

"This isn't funny. We weren't supposed to be locked in," Aiden said to Liam as he saw him. His eyes fell on Teeny, and he frowned. "What happened?"

"Dude, I didn't lock you in," Liam said. He reached over and pulled on the cell door. It didn't budge.

"What the…" Liam's voice trailed off.

Cadence was in the cell with Aiden. The shadowy thing that had been on the ceiling had now moved and was covering the cell door entirely. It looked like it was holding the door in place to trap Aiden inside.

Snow frowned. "Cadence, you need to be careful."

"Really? I thought I wouldn't be," she responded sarcastically. "That's been working so well for me so far. Any ideas, oh, wise one?"

"Working on that. Not entirely sure what it is," Snow answered.

"It looks like the Lexington Hills creature, but it doesn't act like it," Cadence relayed.

"Agreed," Snow confirmed. "But remember, there were several ingredients, so to speak, that went into the make-up of that creature. This could be what Whitfield was describing. Some creature created by bits of souls and sorrows and regrets."

"So, what do I do, Ozzy?" Cade snapped, getting frustrated. "Throw it a party? Send it to therapy? How do I cheer it up to make it go away and let Aiden out?"

Snow frowned. He moved a step toward the cell, then turned and walked into the cell next to the one Cade and Aiden were in. He then walked into the cell to join them.

"Scenic route?" Cade asked.

"I didn't want to give that thing a chance to try to attack," Snow answered.

Aiden had his hands wrapped around the bars of the cell door, through the shadowy creature, and it didn't seem to be affecting him at all. Now both he and Liam were pulling on the door, trying to get it open. The shadows thickened on the side of the cell door where it opened, strengthening itself to hold its prisoner in.

"Wait a minute..." Cadence said as she thought. "Maybe that's it."

"What's it?" Snow asked, perplexed.

Cade flashed Snow a grin that he found both heartening and frightening at the same time. When she smiled, he often disapproved of whatever it was she did next. Cadence walked over to Aiden and put a hand on his back.

Aiden stiffened at the touch, feeling it, but then relaxed as he recognized it. He didn't understand how, since he was not the psychic of their little group, but the words "HAPPY THOUGHTS" kept flashing in his mind. The light touch on his back disappeared as Cadence backed off. Snow moved up to join her, scowling.

"Cadence, what did you just do?" The British accent was clipped as he spoke, indicating his displeasure.

"Oh, relax, Ozzy. If I'm right, I may have just gotten him out of this box." Cadence crossed her arms over her chest and watched Aiden with a smile.

Aiden paused in his pulling and closed his eyes. Images came to his mind of hanging out and joking with Lauren and Derrick. Getting his new apartment. Times with Bethany when they were just together. Videos from the internet he had found hysterical. The shadows on the door began to pull away, retreating from the person conveying such happiness. Their grip on the cell door loosened and then failed entirely as they fled back up to the ceiling.

The cell door opened with a loud clang as both Aiden and Liam shoved it back, having both been pulling on it with all their might. Aiden wasted no time in grabbing the equipment he had put on the floor by the door and getting out of the cell.

"How did you manage that?" Liam asked. "That door was not budging."

"Maybe it just got stuck, and we both put in enough effort to get it unstuck." Aiden shrugged. He sure as hell was not going to try to explain what had just happened, since he didn't understand the entire thing himself. He had no idea why Cade had told him to think happy thoughts at a locked or stuck door. He was even less sure of why it had worked.

"Now might be a good time to regroup and set up the experiment," Liam said.

Teeny wiped the last of the tears from her eyes and face, careful of her make-up, and nodded. "Yeah. I could use a break after that."

"Me, too," Aiden said.

"How did you know?" Snow asked as he and Cadence followed the breathers out of the corridor that held solitary confinement and death row.

"Know what?" Cadence asked with a smile.

"How did you know to tell him whatever it was you told him?" Snow reiterated.

"Well, we were working on the theory that it is what Whitfield said it is, a creature made up of bits of souls, their regrets, their depression and desperation, anger and fear, those are all negative emotions," Cadence started.

"Yes," Snow said with a nod.

"So, I told him to think happy thoughts. The antithesis of what the creature was." Cadence shrugged and smiled at Snow. "I got lucky it worked."

"Indeed." Snow nodded.

CHAPTER 21

The Disappearance

The rustling and clanking of various things being shoved around in a drawer could be heard as the light of a video camera came on. Doug found the flashlight he had been feeling in the kitchen drawer for just after that. Robin and Lauren took the flashlight from Doug and ran up the stairs as the men followed, using the light of the camera. Through the windows by the front door, Derrick had time to notice that the streetlights were on and lights in the neighbors' houses were on. It was just this house that was dark.

"Ava," Robin called as she reached the top of the stairs. "We're coming."

Sam was ahead of them all, having teleported up to the room when the power went out. The darkness didn't affect his vision like it did the others. But even he was too late. Ava was gone, as was Emma. The door of the bedroom opened, and Robin ran in along with Lauren, followed by Doug and Derrick. They all saw the same thing—a child's bedroom in the dark with no child in it.

Robin went over to the bed while Doug went to the closet, both calling out for their daughter. "Ava, where are you, honey?" They checked every conceivable hiding place in the room before beginning to scour the other upstairs rooms. Sam stayed in the little girl's room, hoping to find some clue of where she had been taken, as he knew that Emma had somehow managed to teleport Ava somewhere.

"Sarah?" he called out, frustrated that he was finding no clue left behind. The little girl came out of the open closet, holding her hands in front of her defensively.

"I didn't do it!"

"I know you didn't take Ava," Sam said, getting down on his knees to be face-to-face with the child. "Emma did. But do you know where she took her?"

"There are a lot of places around here that Emma likes to go," Sarah said, her voice small and afraid.

"I know Emma was up here when the lights went out. Did you do something to the power so she could get away?"

"No. That was the man who did that."

"The man? What man?" Sam was confused, as this had been the first time a man had been brought up.

"He's alive, but he knows about spirits. He's the one who summoned Emma back. I think that since I am kind of tied to Emma, I came back, too," Sarah said, shrugging her thin shoulders.

Sam rocked back on his heels a little, his mind working. There was a living man who summoned the girls. He also was here and cut the power to the house so that Emma could make a getaway with the child. But what was all of this really about?

"Sarah, I want to help you, but I need you to help me, too. Do you think you can do that?" Sam's green eyes looked straight into the little girl's big brown ones.

Sarah was slow to nod her head as she was not used to trusting people, but she did nod her head, agreeing to help.

"Thank you, sweetheart," Sam said, hearing the breathers still moving around the house calling for Ava. "When the man summoned you and Emma, did he give you instructions?"

"Not me. I don't know that he knew I was there," Sarah said.

"Okay, did you hear any of the instructions he gave to Emma?"

"Some of it," Sarah said. "He wanted her to find Ava and make friends with her."

"Did he mention Ava in particular," Sam asked, "or did he just say to find another child?"

"He gave Emma this address and told her how to find it," Sarah said. "I don't think he gave her Ava's name, but I could be wrong. I could have just not heard that part. I have to stay a few steps away from Emma, or she gets mad at me."

"Okay, so this address in particular," Sam said, putting that piece of the puzzle aside in his mind. "Did he say why he wanted this child befriended?"

"Not that I know of, and I don't think Emma ever asked, either. She was just too happy to be free."

"You said the same man was here earlier. Did he talk to her then?" Sam was trying to figure out why this family had been targeted by a living person who could obviously summon spirits to do his bidding.

"I'm pretty sure he did," Sarah said. "I found her outside with him, but I think they had already finished talking. She just looked at me and grinned like she was up to somethin' and then went back inside. The guy hung around, and I was keepin' an eye on him, but he just kept an eye on his wristwatch. When it hit a certain time, I think, that's when he cut the power."

Sam nodded as he thought, looking at the carpet as his mind worked the problem over. The breathers were still searching the house, their voices becoming louder and more frantic as they called for Ava to come out from wherever she may be hiding. He had some important puzzle pieces; he knew that, but he just wasn't sure where they fit yet. He also had a feeling that they fit into a much larger puzzle than just what was going on here. Everything going on here seemed a little too deliberate.

"Sarah, where were you and Emma summoned to when the man first brought you back?" An idea had occurred to Sam, and he hoped he was right.

"I think it's where the house we lived in was," Sarah said. "Everything's changed so much I can't be sure. But since that's where we died, it would make sense that's where we were summoned from, right? It wasn't a boneyard."

"Was it in the woods? Was it a house like this one?" He figured it was a good bet that Emma had taken Ava back to where she was summoned. Especially given the fact that whoever the man was that had brought the girls back from the other side was involved.

"It was gonna be a house, I think," Sarah said. "But it wasn't done. It was being built still."

"Could you lead me back to it so I can help these people find their daughter?"

Sarah frowned and looked doubtful. "Miss Emma will be real mad at me."

"Yeah, well, little Miss Emma needs to not be doing what she's been doing," Sam said in reply. "Can you lead me to the place?"

Lauren walked back into the room, her presence startling Sarah.

"Sam, are you here?" Lauren's voice was barely audible in the room.

"Yeah," Sam said, opening the connection between them. "Emma took Ava out of the house. I'm working on finding out where. Be ready to go looking. I'll let you know as soon as I can."

Lauren nodded and left the room, going back downstairs to comfort Robin and to get Derrick ready to leave. Sam turned back to Sarah.

"I know Emma scares you, Sarah," he said. "But she can't hurt you anymore. You're both dead. You're free from her if you want to be. Ava's mom is scared of Emma, too. And right now, Emma has Ava and I'm willing to bet Ava is scared out of her mind since she doesn't know where she is. Please, please help us end this. Take me to where the man summoned you and Emma."

Sarah nodded, struck with the realization that he was right. She wasn't Emma's slave anymore. She didn't have to follow her around and do as she was told. She was free from Emma. Sarah's small fists clenched and her jaw set in a stubborn look as anger began to replace fear in the little girl's eyes.

"Come with me," she said as she reached out for Sam's hand. Sam took the offered hand and the two ghosts teleported away from the Owens' house.

CHAPTER 22

The Experiment

The lobby of the prison was lit with battery-operated lanterns and a couple of lighting rigs for filming. The white light and the grey concrete combined to give the room an otherworldly pale blue hue. Teeny sat on one of the old chairs, hugging her legs to her chest as she rocked back and forth slightly in the chair. Liam stood behind her, his hands on her shoulders, trying to comfort her. Aiden stood a few feet away, letting the two have their time. He busied himself with changing all the batteries, making sure everything was as charged up as possible. Snow and Cadence stayed closer to Liam and Teeny, concern evident in both of their expressions.

"Where the hell was Roy during all of that?" Cadence asked, and it was not the first time she had voiced the question.

"I wish I knew," Snow said in his disapproving tone.

"I wish I knew, too. How the hell did he get to be monitor if he isn't going to do his damned job?" Cadence was pacing the floor, her hands shoved into her pockets.

"Well, the previous officers in this region were obviously a bit lax when it came to this place. Mr. Pruitt even said as much. Perhaps their relaxed approach affected Mr. Pruitt's own approach to his job," Snow offered.

"Something's not right, Snow. You know it. I know you can feel it as much as I do," Cadence said, still pacing.

"Yes, well, it doesn't matter what we feel in our gut, so to speak," Snow said, drawing a scowl from Cadence. "While we can go back and make a case to have Mr. Pruitt removed from his position as a monitor, we do still have a job to do here right now."

"Are you ready to talk about it?" Liam asked, still gently rubbing Teeny's shoulders.

"There's not much to say," Teeny said. Her tears had stopped, but the tracks of the tears down her face remained.

Aiden walked over to them, handing Teeny a bottle of water. "Can you take us through what happened?" He hunkered down beside her, looking up at her and Liam. "From the time you got in there until he got you out."

Teeny took the water bottle Aiden gave her and fiddled with it in her hands. After giving a heavy sigh, she nodded. "Fine. I went in and did the usual sweep of the room with the EMF detector. There was a small spike in the far corner. I went to the middle of the room and just sat down. I thought maybe whatever was there might communicate with me if I was seated, you know? Less threatening."

Liam and Aiden exchanged glances, but neither piped up to tell her that at her diminutive height and size, she was about as threatening as a floating feather.

"I had the recorder going for an EVP session, and a camera pointed toward where I was getting the EMF spike from," she continued. "I was asking questions, and at one point, I thought I heard a growl, then a high-pitched kind of laugh." Teeny shivered a bit, more from the recollection of the sound than from the cold.

"For a long while after that, it was silent," she said, after taking a sip from the water bottle. "I asked questions, have no idea if I got any answers on the tape yet. But there was nothing audible. About ten minutes later, there was a shift in the room. It felt more oppressive, and I could hear scratching on the walls."

"Like rats?" Liam was trying to find a rational explanation, in part to help calm his partner so they could continue with the investigation.

"That's what I thought at first, too," Teeny said. "The scratching got louder, more frantic. It was coming from the corner that the EMF spike was in. I started to get up to go over there, but then … it was like there was this heavy weight on me all of a sudden. I couldn't get up. I couldn't move. It almost felt like there was someone on me, holding me. That's when I started hearing it."

"Hearing what?" Aiden and Liam both asked the question in unison.

"A voice. A male voice, but it was high-pitched, like he was scared or frantic. He was talking fast. I couldn't understand it at first. Then when I could figure out what he was saying..."

"What?" Liam asked, prodding her on.

"...I wish I hadn't understood what he was saying. It was gibberish. Crazy gibberish. But it had to do with blood and trains and portals to other places and people disappearing, but they weren't taking him with them. And shadows. A lot about shadows. That they would eat me, that they would get me. The shadows would keep me here. He said he was still alone. He wanted to keep me there, so he wouldn't be alone, and then the voice went into how he would kill me." Tears fell once more from Teeny's eyes as her voice wavered.

"Shh, it's okay Teeny," Liam said. "He can't hurt you. It's just the ghost of some crazy old man who died here, miserable and alone. Don't let it get under your skin."

Aiden wanted to argue with Liam about ghosts not being able to harm you, but he knew that it wouldn't help the situation at all. Instead, he reached out and patted Teeny gently on the arm. "It's okay. Liam and I won't let anything happen to you."

"Why don't you rest here while Aiden and I move the box into the rotunda, like you wanted?" Liam was hoping his suggestion would spur his partner back into action. He knew she was dying to test out her latest experiment.

"If you think I am letting you leave me somewhere in this godforsaken place by myself, you have another thing coming," Teeny said, the light in her eyes as she answered him one of determination.

"So, coming with us then," Aiden said, and she nodded in response.

"Alright then, let's get this baby situated and up and running," Liam said with a smile.

"We still also have to get to the gallows," Teeny said, her commitment to the investigation strengthening as she shook off the after-effects of the freaky whispers she had endured in solitary confinement. "But I think we should try this first."

Snow and Cadence followed the three investigators as the two men carried the heavy box into the rotunda. It was the size of a large dog crate, with a thick metal bottom and then thick Plexiglas on the remaining five sides. All corners were connected to copper tubing and copper wires that were embedded into the floor of the box.

"I really don't like the look of that." Snow frowned.

"It's experimental tech, probably just some lights and sounds for the audience," Cadence said. "What's got you so wigged out about it?"

"Why are you so convinced that it won't work?" Snow countered.

"This is a television show," Cadence scoffed. "Given our job to make spirits behave, they can't get a ton of material that's exciting enough to put on TV. They have to spice it up, add a little 'ooh and ahh' element to the show. That's all this is. It's Hollywood bullshit."

"And if it works?" Snow was not letting up. "You are letting your living denial about our existence color your perspective, Cadence. You are assuming this is all theatrical when you now know for a fact that it is real. That we are real."

"Yeah, but do you think that they believe that?" Cadence still wasn't sure why Snow was so bothered by this fancy box.

"You know, for a fact, that Aiden does," Snow said, crossing his arms over his chest.

That stopped her for a moment. "Okay, you have a point. He does. So then please explain to me why you think this box could be such a danger."

Snow nodded, pleased that he at least had her listening now, instead of denying things right off the bat. "To me, it almost looks like she has built a kind of Faraday cage, but not quite."

"Faraday cage?" Cadence had no idea what Snow was talking about.

Snow frowned for a moment as he tried to figure out how to explain it to her. "Alright, have you ever seen one of those large Tesla coils that has metal cages around them?"

"You mean like the mad scientist lab kind of thing, with the electricity arcing out of it and zapping the cage around it?"

"Yes." Snow nodded. "That's a Faraday cage. It's designed to trap and ground electromagnetic energy within the cage's confines so that it doesn't escape."

"Okay ... But if it traps what's inside of there, what danger is it to us? I don't see either one of us volunteering to go sit inside the thing," Cadence questioned. She made a quick sidestep closer to Snow as Liam passed through where she had just been, rolling a generator in with him. She then pointed a finger at Snow, who was smiling at her with amusement. "Not a word. Yes, I know he can walk through me. It still feels damned weird, and I don't like it, so just shut up about it."

"I didn't say a word," Snow said, though his tone and expression were both filled with amusement.

"Trust me, you don't have to; your face is speaking loudly enough," Cade grumbled.

"You really should try to get used to it," Snow suggested.

"I don't want to get used to it," Cadence complained. "It feels really freaky to have someone just walk through me. You've had fifty years to get used to all this crap. I haven't. So, go on about the Faraday thing and let me have my pet peeves in peace."

"As you wish," he acquiesced, but his mouth was still curved into a smile. "As I was saying, the Faraday cage is designed to trap energy within it. Normally, this wouldn't be an issue to us out here, but I have no idea what adjustments she may have made to the design to try to draw in energy."

"So, she could have altered the design to draw in and trap ghosts?" Cadence wanted to make sure she understood what Snow was saying.

"It is possible, yes." Snow nodded. "It also is possible that it is something just for theatrics, as you said. But from what I can see, the science behind the design is sound."

"When did you get into all this science stuff?" Cadence asked, eyeing the box as the breathers connected the generator to it.

"I have interests in many things, Cadence. And as you said, I have had a few decades to learn," Snow said with a smile.

"What do you think we should do, then?" Cade asked, as the generator came to life with a loud growl.

"Stay well away from it, just in case," Snow replied. "Hopefully, you are right and I am wrong, and it is just some light and mirror trick for television. If I am right, and we stay out of its field of energy, we should be safe enough."

"Safe ... enough? That's not exactly inspiring, you know," Cadence said. Her gaze was drawn to one side as Roy appeared near Snow. "Where on earth have you been?"

Snow turned, a little startled at the monitor's sudden appearance. "She's quite right. You've been missing since the fracas in the solitary confinement and death row corridor."

"The natives were gettin' restless," Roy said in his southern accent. "Tryin' to convince them to settle down and not come out to mess with the breathers is a job of work."

"Where are they all?" Cadence asked as something occurred to her. "I mean, we saw those few in the cafeteria, a couple down the death row corridor, but not so many as would require you to be away all that time."

Roy narrowed his eyes at Cadence. "Look here, sugar. You don't tell me how to do my job, and I won't tell you how to do yours. That work fer you, sweetheart?"

"If you don't cut out the sexist bullshit, you'll find out how much it doesn't work for me," Cadence said, moving toward him. "I've put up with the sexism and the disrespect because of when you died, how things were back then. But I am done with it. All this time, you have pretty much just shown us how crappy you are at your job. So, if you would please at least show me the modicum of respect I am due for my position, if nothing else, I would appreciate it."

Snow didn't interrupt Cadence's tirade. Much as he usually tried to keep her hot-headedness in check, she was right.

Roy looked to Snow for help. "Think you need to rein that filly in there, Snow."

Cade drew back to punch Roy in his mustachioed face but drew up short when, to her surprise, Snow beat her quite literally to the punch. Roy rocked back, stunned, and held his hand to his mouth, looking at Snow with wide eyes. He took his hand away to reveal a trickle of silvery blood from the corner of his mouth.

There was a strange beat where time seemed to stand still as the machine behind them was turned on. A pulse of energy went through the room, and it was like every inch of Cade's skin was suddenly crawling. She could see that Snow and Roy felt it, too. Snow shook out his hand, as it was tingling as if it had fallen asleep.

"I think it's best we take this elsewhere," Snow said. "This machine is "

"How about you take yourself in there?" Roy interrupted, grabbing Snow by both shoulders and shoving him toward the machine.

"Snow!" Cadence yelled, and her voice echoed enough that the breathers heard her. She reached out, trying to catch him, but Roy intercepted her, grabbing her and throwing her in the opposite direction.

"Now hows about you sit yerself down and shut up," Roy growled. He then turned on his heel and disappeared from the room.

Snow had fallen backward at the shove, and it was apparent Teeny's science had been as spot-on as Snow's explanation of it. Snow had fallen into the large box, which had filled with a blue glow. There was a snap and Cadence found, as she sat on the floor against the opposite wall where Roy had thrown her, that her skin didn't feel like it was crawling anymore. A light on the console of controls attached to the bottom of the box began to blink.

"Holy shit, we got one," Teeny whispered, her voice barely above a breath, as if speaking out loud would break the spell, and it would all have been for nothing.

"No. Snow." Cadence struggled to her feet, her lower legs and feet stinging from the action.

Snow was kneeling within the glowing blue light of the box. Cade could see him, but it was like there was an electrical storm inside the box with him. He jerked as one of the arcs of lightning hit him in the back, wincing as another hit his arm.

Teeny hit a couple of buttons on the box and turned a dial. The lightning in the box increased, and the blue fog got brighter before both began to dissipate. Snow's form, looking like it was made of the nebulous fog that had filled the box, was visible to the breathers.

"You did it, Teeny," Liam said in awe, his eyes wide.

Aiden's eyes were locked on the box as well, but his face didn't reflect victory or even happiness. He was horror-stricken, as he knew exactly who was in the box. He glanced around, looking for any sign of Cadence or any of the others who so often were with Snow. How on earth was he supposed to get these guys to bury this footage?

Cadence took a step toward the box, and Snow quickly held up a hand, indicating she should stop.

"How," Liam said, copying the movement that had been interpreted by 1950s cinema as a greeting for Native Americans.

Teeny elbowed Liam in the leg since he was standing and she was kneeling on the floor at the controls for the box. "Does he look like a Native American to you? Idiot." She shook her head.

"Ow," Liam said. "You have bony elbows, lady."

Cadence stayed where she was, but her mind was going a mile a minute. She had to find a way to get him out of there. They had to find a way to scrub the footage. And they had a serious bone to pick with Roy Pruitt.

"What do you think, Aiden? Is he an inmate or what?" Liam asked.

"He's not wearing a prisoner's uniform, at least from the pictures of inmates we saw," Aiden said. "He's also not wearing a guard's uniform."

"Maybe a visitor who happened to be in the wrong place at the wrong time during one of the riots," Teeny suggested.

"It's possible, but only one of the riots resulted in civilian deaths. He doesn't look like he's from that time," Liam said.

"You're awfully quiet, Aiden," Teeny said. "What do you think?"

"I'm not sure," he said, moving toward the box. His mind was whirling with ideas to explain this away or to simply cut the experiment short. His immediate plan was to "trip" over the power wire from the generator. He hoped it would yank the power supply from the machine at least long enough to let Snow get out of the damned thing.

"Oh, hey, careful," Liam said, putting out a hand to pause Aiden in his tracks. "Careful of the cord."

Aiden could only nod in response. *Well, fuck, there goes that plan*, he thought to himself.

"Can you hear me?" Teeny looked at Snow as she asked this. They could see Snow's eyes moving as he looked around, but so far, he had yet to try to move or communicate.

Cadence knew Snow was deliberately quiet, to not have his voice recorded. The spirit box freaked him out enough; she knew he would in no way want to give these television show people his voice. She looked on helplessly as she tried to think of a way to get him out.

An angry, hungry howl sounded from down the corridor that housed the gallows. The breathers heard it, too, as they all looked up from the box to the pitch-black hallway. Aiden shivered, feeling the hairs on his neck rise.

"Maybe we should let him soak up some of the energy in there before we try to communicate with him," Liam said, his eyes locked on the hallway the growl had come from.

"I can stay with the box," Aiden offered, seeing his opportunity to set Snow free. "You two should probably check that out."

"Teeny knows how to work the box. I want her to stay with it," Liam said.

"I don't want to stay here alone, though," Teeny said in protest. "Not after solitary confinement."

"So, you and Aiden stay here. I'll go check out that sound," Liam said.

"Yes, because hurrying off on your own in a dark, abandoned prison is such a good idea. Surely nothing bad will happen," Teeny said, sarcasm dripping heavily from her voice. "Just wait for this to be done and then we can go to the gallows room together. That's where that sound came from, right?"

"Yep, that's where it sounded like it came from. I can handle myself, and you know it," Liam said. "You two just hang out here and see if you can get Mr. Fancy-Pants here to talk or communicate somehow."

"Liam, the rule is we never go off on our own," Teeny said. "You know that. So no one is ever alone if something bad happens, like in solitary."

"Bro, are you sure you don't want company?" Aiden asked. He knew that if his chance to sabotage the box was out, he may as well accompany Liam and try to keep him safe.

"Nah, I'm good," Liam said with a smile and a nonchalant shrug. "Thanks, anyway." Grabbing his gear, Liam turned and headed down the hallway. Cadence followed him, as she knew there was little she could do for Snow right now, and she could at least try to protect Liam from the dangers he didn't believe in.

CHAPTER 23

Finding More Than They Bargained For

The streetlights had yet to reach this part of the neighborhood development. Most lots were either still being built or were just bulldozed and awaiting construction crews. The site that Sarah teleported Sam to had the wooden frame of the house being built, as well as the sheathing, but no doors or windows had been fitted in yet. The dirt yard had piles of various supplies, and the dull glint of metallic nails and screws, dropped by those who had once carried them, glinted in the moonlight. A few weeds here and there tried to push their way through the cold hard ground.

"Here?" Sam looked down at Sarah, an eyebrow raised.

Sarah nodded and, without a word, lifted her arm to point at the house. Sam found the gesture incredibly eerie. He shook off the creepiness and headed inside. Mentally, he reached out to Lauren, using his connection with her as a kind of homing beacon. They were too far away to speak mind to mind, but she would feel a pull toward him, and that would guide her here. He felt the spark on the other end of their connection. He knew from that spark that she felt the pull and recognized it.

The wooden walls were up, and some duct work was piled in the corner of a room. There was no paint, plaster, or tile to make this skeletal house inviting. It smelled like dirt and wood. The roof was on, which protected the items left inside from the elements. However, it gave more shadows for things to hide in. The dimness would make it more difficult for the breathers to see and would make them more reliant on their flashlights. That might make things more dangerous if the breather that Sarah had talked about was involved in this.

He could hear the murmuring of a child's voice talking, though he couldn't make out the words being said. He made his way in, following the sound past the staircase that led up to the second level, around a corner, and through an open door into a large room. Ava was there, huddled in a far corner of the room, with Emma standing between her and the doorway. The ghostly child had her hands on her hips.

"I told you, you can't go yet," Emma said. "We gotta wait on the wolf to get here."

"Don't wolves eat children?" Ava asked, her voice small and quivering with fear.

Emma laughed. "No, silly!" She was still acting like everything was just fine, and they were two friends talking. "He's a living man who is gonna help me out."

"If he's helping you, why do you need me?" Ava was scared and confused by all of this, and it showed in her voice and on her face.

"I need you because you're who he asked me to get, you goose!" Emma chuckled and shook her head for a moment. "My Mama always used to call me that when I was silly. She would say I was bein' a goose."

"Please, Emma, please, I wanna go home. I'm scared. Momma and daddy are probly scared," Ava cried.

"I can't let you go, goose," Emma said again. "Wolf is gonna make me into you so I can be real again."

"Let her go, Emma," Sam said, taking a couple steps closer to Emma. Sarah moved to stand beside him, offering him silent support.

Emma turned, startled. She looked at Sam with wide eyes, but then she saw Sarah and her eyes narrowed.

"I shoulda known you would go an' try to ruin this for me," Emma accused, taking a step away from Ava and moving toward Sarah with menace and hatred in her eyes. "You always try to ruin my fun."

"Your fun is causing pain to others," Sarah said, getting the guts to step forward and stand against Emma. "You can't do that. It's not right."

"I can do whatever I like to those lesser'n me. It's my God-given right," Emma replied.

"No," Sam said, finally speaking up. "It isn't. It never was. Taking your anger and jealousy out on people when you were alive was evil. I can't put it plainer than that."

Emma drew herself up to look very self-important. "My Granddaddy says "

"It doesn't matter what he said, Emma," Sam said. "He's been dead and gone for a long time. His view of the world was wrong. What he taught you was wrong, and I honestly doubt he meant for his words to be taken to the extremes you've taken them to."

Emma looked like she couldn't decide between breaking down into tears or going into a fearsome rage. She was visibly trembling, her lips drawn in a tight, thin line as her chin quivered. That was when Ava stepped forward.

"Emma, I know you're alone. I can be your friend if you stop being scary and bossy," the little girl said. "No one can make you me. No one can make you alive."

Footsteps on the wooden boards of the floor sounded, and Sam wondered if Derrick and Lauren had caught up to them yet. A solid dark form moved into the doorframe and then passed through it. The moonlight through the windows revealed that this person was not who Sam had hoped for. But he did recognize the man. After all the years he had spent watching over his sister, he knew the face of this man well.

The man was of average height. He had a sharp nose and an angular face, as if his visage had been chiseled from rock. Dark eyes were set in a tan face that was clean-shaven. He wore a dark wool trench coat over dark pants and work boots. A dark knit cap covered his head.

The three girls and Sam watched as the man made his way into the room. Ava instinctively took a step back for every step forward the man took. Sarah frowned, Emma smiled, and Sam wondered if this person was going to end up being a bigger problem than he could deal with.

"Wolf!" Emma greeted the man with enthusiasm.

"Good job, little one," Wolf said as he stalked across the room to where Ava cowered. "You've brought her right where I told you to."

"Course I did," Emma said. "I ain't no ninny." Emma stood as straight as she could with her hands on her hips, as if to challenge the idea that she wouldn't do what she promised.

Wolf looked over to the little ghost girl and just lifted an eyebrow. That single look spoke louder than any yell as to what he actually thought of the child's prowess. He then looked back at Ava. "Now … What to do with you now that you are here?"

"Let me go?" Ava suggested, though her voice trembled as she spoke.

Wolf's head rolled back as laughter erupted from him. Sam and Sarah edged closer to Ava. "You are going to be a delight, aren't you?" Wolf asked.

"You said you knew how to make me into her so I could be real again," Emma said. Her tone made it unclear whether she was reminding Wolf of his promise or demanding it from him. She caught sight of Sarah and Sam edging closer and stomped her foot. "Stop it," Emma said in a hiss through clenched teeth as she reached over, past Wolf, and grabbed Sarah by the dress, dragging the girl over to her. "You'll get us into trouble!"

Wolf finished laughing and looked back at Ava, shaking his head. "No. Sorry, kiddo. You don't get to go. At least not yet. You're too good a distraction." There was an air of quiet menace to this man that made Sam worry. He had no doubt that this man could follow through on any threat he made without batting an eyelash. Of course, he also knew that this Wolf fellow had been involved with one of his minions' attempts to kill a cop a few weeks ago, so that likely added to his unease. As did the fact that he knew exactly who this Wolf person was.

Wolf looked at Emma with thinly disguised contempt. "You get to go nowhere. You can't really have thought I was going to let a sociopath like you get a second chance at living."

"But you promised me." Emma stamped her foot so hard that her brown curls bounced.

"A promise made to a gullible, spoiled brat holds no water," Wolf said. "You fetched what I wanted you to fetch. I'll put you away shortly."

Sam pulled on that connection he had to Lauren, and he could tell she was closer than she had been. He only hoped they could get here in time because while he could handle Emma, he wasn't sure what tricks this Wolf guy had up his sleeve.

Wolf hunkered down to be eye level with Ava and held out his hand. "You'll leave here alive if you're a good girl. Now, let me see that hand of yours," Wolf said. He was deliberate in ignoring Emma, much to the girl's annoyance.

Ava was visibly trembling as she did as she was told and held out her hand to the man. Her eyes darted to each of the ghosts, as if pleading with them to make this end. Fresh tears were streaming down her cheeks, but she cried silently, too afraid of Wolf to make a noise.

Wolf examined the girl's hand and forearm, running his black leather gloved fingers over her smooth skin. "Perfect," he said, his voice quiet. "You and I have a lot in common, Ava. I'm sorry this is scary for you. But you'll get to know that I'm not as scary as all of this." A few houses away, a dog began barking. Wolf looked up, listening to the sound, then looked at Emma.

"Emma, are we the only ones here? You, me, and the girl?" Wolf's dark eyes were hard as he looked at the ghost girl.

"Well, Sarah is here. She's always with me, though," Emma said with a shrug, looking down at her shoes. She was getting the feeling that Wolf was perhaps trying to shirk his promise to bring her back to the land of the living.

"Emma!" Wolf's voice was like the crack of a whip through the quiet, unfinished house.

"Well, I dunno how he followed me," Emma said, backing away from Wolf a bit.

"Who?" Wolf's tone made it more of a demand than a question.

"I never bothered to get his name. It's the young man that follows that lady around." Emma was trying to backpedal quickly, knowing that Sam's presence there was upsetting Wolf.

Wolf sighed and closed his eyes for a moment, centering himself. Sarah took the opportunity to grab Ava and teleported her down to the basement of the house. Sarah wasn't strong enough to teleport a living human too far, but she knew that would buy Ava at least a few more minutes away from Wolf. Emma yelped as Sarah and Ava disappeared suddenly, her yelp coinciding with a scream from beneath them in the basement.

Wolf, once centered, opened his eyes. Looking around the room, he found Sam. "A white knight for the young princess, huh?" he said. "What do you think you can do here, boy? I can do far more damage to you than you can to me."

"I guess we'll just have to see about that," Sam said with a shrug.

Wolf gave a slight wave of his hand, and the wounds that had killed Sam when he was mortal shimmered to life. Sam flinched, not prepared to feel the sting, but there was no blood, just light.

"Recognizable handiwork," Wolf said. "It's curious that you ended up here. I guess it doesn't matter in the end. You still can't stop me." Wolf knew exactly who the spirit of the young man was.

"Stop you from doing what?" Sam looked over to see Emma had taken the opportunity to flee as well while Wolf's attention was on him. "What is this child to you? Why go to such lengths?"

Wolf chuckled and turned, as if dismissing Sam. He froze when he saw Ava was gone. His body went rigid, and his face flushed with anger. He whirled back to Sam, and Sam could feel the anger radiating out of him almost as palpable as he had felt the menace earlier.

"Where is she?" Wolf demanded.

"I was busy talking to you." Sam shrugged nonchalantly, though he was ready to move quickly if needed. "How should I know? I guess that's why they say you should always keep an eye on your kids, right? They can disappear in the blink of an eye."

"You people need to stay the hell out of my business. That goes for you and the living you work with," Wolf said, his voice nearly a growl. With that, he turned and began striding for the door.

Sam could feel that Lauren was almost there. If they could call the cops and get Wolf arrested for kidnapping, that might put a big dent in whatever nefarious plan he had going on. But if he left or worse, took Ava elsewhere, there would be little hope.

"That's not what you told Mike Caulfield." It was Sam's Hail Mary play, to try to shock Wolf into stopping, into forgetting what he was about to do. It worked.

Wolf turned back, his dark eyes glittering with malice in the moonlight. "What do you know of Caulfield?"

"I know he worked for you. I also know he wasn't really Caulfield." Sam was talking, throwing things out there to try to reel Wolf in, get him to stay in place.

"That's why I said the handiwork of your death is recognizable. I know who you are, Samuel Riley," Wolf said. Wolf was gratified to see a look of shock cross Sam's face.

"How do you know who I am?" Sam was genuinely flat-footed at that revelation, and he was scrambling to try to figure out how the man knew him.

"Please," Wolf said, waving a hand dismissively. "The massacre at the college was big news. And we've already established that you and I both know about Caulfield."

"But it was ten years ago. That's a lot of time to pass to remember my face," Sam said.

"Photographic memory," Wolf said, tapping his temple with a black, leather-clad finger. "It's a gift and a curse. Now stop stalling and tell me where those two vaporous twits hid the girl."

"I wouldn't know," Sam said as the sound of an engine roared into the driveway, headlights flashing through the beams of wood still left open. "But I don't think it matters now." Flashing red and blue lights could be seen now, too, as the sound of car doors opening and closing echoed in the quiet night, exciting some nearby dogs again.

"Damn it," Wolf said through clenched teeth. He turned and exited the room in a hurry, making his way toward the back of the house. Footsteps sounded on the floorboards as people made their way quickly inside.

"Ava!" Lauren and Derrick called in unison. Two officers came in behind them, yelling at them that they should be waiting outside. Sam teleported to Lauren and touched her arm, just to make sure the connection was ironclad between them.

"I'm not sure where she is. I think Sarah took her to safety. Wolf made his way out the back," Sam said to her.

"I think I see a guy running away from here that way," Lauren said, and one of the officers dutifully ran in the direction she pointed, the way Wolf had gone. The other officer stayed behind with Lauren and Derrick.

Sarah appeared beside Sam and tugged on his elbow. Sam turned and knelt down. "Is she safe?"

"She's in the basement. She's cold, and she stepped on a nail, but she's okay," Sarah said.

"Basement," Sam said to Lauren through their connection, and she relayed that to the officer. The three breathers then hurried to find the way downstairs. Sarah and Sam teleported down to the little girl, who was huddled in a corner behind the stairs. Her foot had a carpenter's nail clean through the middle of it, and she was doing her best to be as quiet as she could in spite of the pain. Emma was there as well, looking genuinely remorseful and guilty. As footsteps came down the stairs, Ava seemed to draw in on herself, as if trying to pull back further into the shadows.

"Ava?" Lauren called out.

The girl let out a sob of relief. "Here!" she called, recognizing Lauren's voice. Lauren, Derrick, and the officer rounded the staircase and were visibly relieved to see the girl was alive and, for the most part, unharmed. The officer radioed for an ambulance and to the officers who were apparently stationed at the house with Robin and Doug that their daughter had been found. Derrick took off his coat and put it around Ava.

"He wasn't gonna do what he said," Emma said in disbelief.

Sam looked over at the little southern belle. "You sound surprised."

"Gentlemen don't make promises and not keep 'em," Emma said, her confusion genuine.

"Emma," Sam said with a sigh, "I told you before. The world doesn't work the way it used to anymore."

"But a promise is a promise," Emma argued.

"Not anymore. Nowadays, people can lie at the drop of a hat and not care," Sam said.

"Or maybe he wasn't a gentleman," Sarah said, her voice soft.

"I'm tired," Emma said after a moment. "And I don't like the way your world works," she added, looking at Sam.

"Do you want to go back to your rest?" Sam knew who he could send the girls to if that was the case. And Bethany Saxon could see to it that they were both safe, that Wolf couldn't summon them again.

"No," Emma said, after thinking about it for a minute. "I wanna get the wolf for lying to me. Come on, Sarah, we're going."

"I'm not going," Sarah said.

Emma's jaw dropped in shock as Sarah so openly defied her. "What do you mean? Of course, you are. I said so."

"No. I don't belong to you anymore," Sarah said. "I don't have to do what you say."

Emma narrowed her eyes and looked from Sarah to Sam. "Fine. I'll get the wolf for lyin', and you for taking her away from me." Emma Barton then disappeared with one last furious glower.

"Can you send me back to wherever I was before that man summoned us?" Sarah's brown eyes were hopeful.

"I know someone who can," Sam said with a smile, offering Sarah his hand.

CHAPTER 24

Captured Evidence

Snow was fuming. He sat in the large box contraption, unable to get out of it, and in plain view of the two breathers and their cameras. He was silently but vehemently chastising himself for not having caught onto Mr. Pruitt and his intentions sooner. He should have known that the man wasn't off tending to his charges. He should have followed his and Cadence's gut instincts that something was terribly off. But the information they had about the prison itself made him chalk up their misgivings to the natural unpleasantness left over from so many lives taken violently here over the years.

Snow's only consolation was the fact that Aiden was a good man. He trusted the breather to do his best to either damage or hide the video evidence or perhaps come up with some story to say it was all smoke and mirrors concocted by the television duo for their show. And so he sat silently, angry at himself and the situation, but not even attempting communication with the breathers despite the woman's repeated tries.

"I don't get it," Teeny said with a sigh. "There should be enough energy built up in there for the ghost to draw on to communicate with us."

"Maybe the guy doesn't want to communicate," Aiden said with a shrug, unable to do much to help Snow yet.

Teeny looked incredulous at such a suggestion. "They always want to communicate. He's got to have questions, why he is there, who we are, things like that."

"Dude just looks kind of pissed off if you ask me," Aiden said, giving Teeny one more shrug of his shoulders.

"Which is more reason for him to be trying to communicate," Teeny said. "Even if he just wants to cuss me out for trapping him in there."

Snow idly entertained the thought of taking a page out of his partner's book and flipping the young lady the bird, but he decided against it. He was determined that while he was stuck in there, he was going to make no move to comply with what she wanted.

Another terrible howl from the gallows yard echoed through the stone halls of the prison, and both breathers and the trapped ghost looked toward the origin of the sound with worry. Snow frowned. If something evil was here and was waking up, as that sound seemed to portend, he needed to get free of this damned cage. Cadence was just back on her feet, not even wholly out of pain yet. He couldn't leave her to handle something like that on her own.

"Do you think Liam's okay?" Teeny asked, her attention focused down the hallway where her partner had disappeared.

"I would guess he is. That sure as hell didn't sound like him yelling for help," Aiden said. He had noticed Snow's movement and guessed his concern but wasn't saying a thing about it to Teeny. In fact, he had moved to stand between the camera and its view of the cage that Snow was caught in while Teeny's attention was diverted.

Snow noticed Aiden's position and the woman's lack of attention. In a swift movement, he tried to punch his arm through the barrier that was holding him inside the box. He used the power that Croft had taught him. It was the power that had let him get Cadence out of the cage and fuse the lock on Overton after Cadence was free. He felt a sharp impact, almost like he had just tried to strike a wall of electrified knives. His hand did not break through the barrier, but it hurt like hell now. The impact sounded like a truck hitting an electric fence.

"Dammit," Snow muttered without thinking. His voice and the sound of his punch got the attention of the breathers once more.

"You can speak," Teeny said in surprise and delight, turning her attention back to her successful experiment. "Please, talk with us. We would like to help you."

Snow cradled his arm, which felt like it had fallen painfully asleep. His head was bowed, and he let it remain so. He still had no intention of talking to them. He did, however, use a little bit of the excess energy being poured into him by the box to form a detective's shield, like Cadence carried, clipped to his belt. Once he could feel it in place, he moved slightly. This adjustment to his position let his blazer fall open a bit, making the shield visible. This did not go unnoticed by Teeny.

"Aiden, I think you were right," she said, leaning forward, closer to the box to see. "Look, it looks like he has a police badge."

"Derrick did say there were a couple of riots here over the years," Aiden said. "It's reasonable that a cop could have been here during one, just got caught in the wrong place at the wrong time while talking to an inmate or something."

"Officer," Teeny said, "please, we just want to try to help you. Please talk with us."

Aiden still had himself positioned between the camera and the box. Of course, he had no fix for the camera he was wearing, having gotten used to the weight of the straps on his shoulders. He did his best to obscure what he could by crossing his arms over his chest, but that only hid half of the lens.

Snow didn't move or respond to the young woman's pleas for communication.

"Look, officer, I can understand you're confused and upset at this situation," Teeny said, still not yet giving up on communication with the ghost. "My name is Tina. I would love to know your name. We would truly like to learn about you and help you move on." After a few moments of waiting for the spirit to respond but getting nothing, not even any motion from him, Teeny sighed.

"Maybe Liam is having better luck, huh?" Aiden said.

Liam's footsteps echoed in the dark hallway as Cadence walked soundlessly beside him. He was using the night vision on his handheld camera to see as well as record. Why he didn't use a flashlight was beyond Cadence, but it wasn't her decision. The dark didn't bother her, anyway.

"So, I've left Teeny and Aiden with the experiment," Liam said, talking to the camera. He was really just talking to take his attention off of his nerves as he made his way toward the gallows room, but he would never admit that in a million years. "We heard this weird sound coming from out there. I'm not gonna lie, it was kind of a scary sound. But we here at *The Dead Show* don't shy away from the strange and scary."

"Yeah? What about real and terrifying," Cadence said, keeping her voice low enough to be sure it wasn't picked up by the microphones Liam had.

The hinges on the door to the yard were so rusty and disused that they seemed to scream in protest as Liam pushed the door open. The night was cold and quiet. Patches of snow on the ground seemed to sparkle under the dim light of the stars and moon. Out of that peacefulness, the gallows building rose, standing dark against the white snow. Liam stopped and let his camera linger on the two-story building.

"That building is where the people condemned to hang spent their last moments, their last breaths," Liam said. "When the time came for a prisoner to be executed, they would be escorted from death row out to this yard, and this would be the last time they would see the sky, or smell the fresh air."

The same terrible noise that had drawn him out here in the first place came again. Only this time, it was much closer and coming from directly in front of him. Liam took a step back. "I, uh … I'm not sure what's making that noise in there. It's weird sounding, that's for sure. Let's go find out."

"That's your best plan?" Cadence knew she wouldn't get a response to the question, but she had to ask it, anyway. "Let's go find out?" She shook her head in dismay as she followed him. "Idiot."

The doors to the gallows room were chained shut. Liam paused and tucked his camera under an arm as he fished in his coat pockets for the keys to the prison. He tried one after another on the padlock until one finally worked. The doors opened silently, which both Liam and Cadence found to be unnerving. After all of the screeching and protesting of all the other hinges in the prison, how on earth could these have been silent? Especially given the fact that these had been so exposed to the elements, just like the front door had been.

Liam hesitated for a moment, but only that, before he stepped inside the building with Cadence right beside him. To Liam's right was a staircase leading up to a second-floor landing in front of a closed door. To his left was another closed door. In front of him was an unadorned wall. There were brighter spots on the wall, indicating that pictures had hung there for a long time before being taken down. Liam turned left and went through the unlocked door. A small corridor let out into a wide room of seats. The chairs faced a 2-story glass wall. The room beyond the glass was mired in shadow, but with the night vision on the camera, Liam could make out the gallows.

"This must have been where officials and maybe family members of victims or the criminal would come to watch the inmate's final moments. They would sit here as the inmate would be led upstairs and watch as he dropped through the trapdoor to his death," Liam said, his voice quiet.

Cadence looked into the other room through the window-wall and could see what Liam and his camera couldn't. A roiling mass of shadows that seemed to mimic water was in there, all over the room. It would try to rise up in some form or another, but it was dripping bits of itself back to the ground like rain. It reminded her of a less cohesive version of the non-human chaos entity she and Snow had dealt with at Lexington Hills when she had first crossed over. That recognition did nothing to lessen her feeling of dread.

Liam panned the camera around the viewing room slowly. "Okay, let's go check out the gallows," he said with a sigh, mustering his courage to sound more confident than he was. This place was getting to him; he was getting creeped out, but he couldn't let the viewers know that.

"You really don't want to go in there," Cadence said, knowing her voicing her thoughts on the matter was fruitless. She followed him as he retraced his steps out of the viewing room and back to the small entrance.

The stairs were concrete with iron bars for a railing. Liam's footsteps on the stairs made a strange sound. They should have echoed at least a little in the emptiness of the room, but they were barely there. It was like he was walking on carpet instead of concrete. As Liam lifted his feet, Cadence could see more of the inky bits of shadow under his foot before they disappeared back into the concrete. Liam reached the top of the stairs and opened the door to the gallows room.

Cadence went in with him, unwilling to leave the breather unprotected, but if she had had her way, they would not have been in there. Sounds enveloped them as they entered, though she couldn't be sure what Liam could and couldn't hear. There were growls, screams, sobs, all different voices and intonations coming from the shadows and all over the room.

"Jesus," Liam said with a soft breath. "I know you can't feel anything through the television, but this room is incredibly daunting. There is so much anger, so much grief, it's almost suffocating. The feeling in this room is so oppressive and overwhelming."

A thundering sound, like a chorus of voices rising up in an angry, defiant scream, resounded through the room. Liam froze, his eyes widening, confirming to Cadence that he had heard that one.

Cadence looked over at one corner of the room where it seemed the majority of the bits and pieces of shadow kept trying to coalesce and form themselves into something solid. "You guys need to cut this shit out right now. Be quiet. As soon as we leave, you can go back to making noise," she said. She had no idea if the bits of dark souls would have enough sentience to hear and understand her, but she had to try.

"They ain't gonna listen to you, Missy," Roy Pruitt's southern drawl came from the far end of the room, at the ground floor near the window-wall.

"You," Cadence said. Her voice was hard and almost as full of anger and hate as the bits and pieces of souls in the room. She teleported down to the ground level of the building, leaving Liam up on the gallows floor by himself.

Roy smiled as she materialized in front of him. "Having fun in here, darlin'?"

"You need to pray that Snow gets out of that damned box and that we can get the video away from these guys somehow," Cadence said.

"Really?" Roy stepped closer to the glass wall as he said this. "That's the only footage yer worried about?" He smiled and put his arm through the glass. A bluish light shot down his arm from his shoulder to his fingertips, and the glass instantly shattered.

The falling of glass onto concrete was as musical as it was loud in the still room. The suddenness of it made Liam shriek in surprise, and even the shadows backed off as if startled. Liam focused his camera in on where the glass had been and walked closer to the edge of the gallows to get a better view.

"What on earth just happened?" Liam's voice was hushed as he spoke to himself. "This is insane." Panning the camera down, he recorded the bits and pieces of shattered glass that littered the ground floor. The window had been enormous, two stories tall and probably 12 feet wide. The amount of glass it left on the floor was considerable.

Another phantom scream sounded from the shadows. Cadence looked, and their movements seemed more agitated. Liam stopped when he heard the scream.

"Okay, no bullshit, this place is freaking me out," Liam admitted.

"Looks like yer boy there is getting a bit more than he thought he would, huh?" Roy had a smug, satisfied smirk on his face that Cadence wanted to punch. "You wanna play with big boys, Missy? Well, come on an' play then. I'm sure we'll have a great time helpin' you learn yer place."

"Look, you misogynistic piece of shit " Cadence began, but Roy cut her off.

"No, you better look." Roy chuckled and disappeared.

Cadence let out an emphatic grunt of frustration, knowing that even if Liam or his equipment picked up her sound that it would just blend in or be overpowered by the noise of the agitated shadows. She teleported back up to the gallows floor to keep tabs on Liam.

The ghost hunter was backing up from the edge of the gallows, still filming the broken glass and now vacant window area. "I think I caught a light anomaly down there, an orb or two. We'll have to go back over the footage, though, to be sure," he said, talking to his camera again. "This place is insane."

Cadence noticed the shadows out of the corner of her eye. They were getting taller, climbing the far wall as if they were reaching for something. That was when she realized there was a lever on the wall, and it was as if the shadows were trying to reach for it. Looking over at Liam, she saw him back up onto the trapdoor, still immersed in what he saw on his camera's display.

"No!" she shouted, teleporting over to the wall with the lever, but it was too late. In the blink of an eye, the shadows surged and solidified enough to yank the lever down. The floor dropped out from under Liam, and he screamed as he fell to the floor below, landing with an audible crunch.

The shadows moved, trying to lunge toward Cadence now that she was close. They covered her hand, moving up her forearm. It felt like a million spiders had been let loose to crawl on her flesh, but other than tugging on her, they were able to do little before dripping away back to the floor as they had expended most of their coherence and energy to pull the gallows trap. Cadence teleported down to where Liam had fallen beneath the trapdoor as she shook off the remnants of the dark souls.

His right leg was broken, Cadence could tell that immediately. It made a V shape out to the side with his foot facing the wrong way. Blood was beginning to soak through into the fabric of his jeans in a couple of places. The other leg looked more intact, but she had no way of knowing. All she knew was that it wasn't at the grotesque angle his right leg was. The broken glass of the viewing window had scattered all over the floor, and he had some cuts from landing on pieces that she could see. He was breathing; Cadence was thankful for the cold weather making his breath physically apparent.

The shadowy bits of souls, pieces of anger, hate, loss, all began trying to get closer to Liam's body. Cadence moved to stand by the man's head and pulled her knife. The leftovers of criminal souls once more tried to coalesce, to become a shape. Cadence didn't hesitate in moving forward and cutting into the shadowy shape. More howls of anger and pain erupted throughout the room.

"You don't get to have him," Cadence said, her voice forceful. The shadows dripped, formed, and ebbed around her, seeming to almost seethe, until they backed off, slinking their way back to the walls.

Cadence looked down once more at the unconscious ghost hunter. The screen of his handheld camera had shattered. She had no idea if the device was still recording or not, but it was pointed toward the seats and the viewing area. The camera he had strapped to his chest was probably still working just fine, as the plastic case it was in seemed undamaged. She decided to stay where she was, by his head, and hoped she was well enough out of the camera's view because she was going to have to use some energy.

She sat down on the floor, unbothered by the bits of broken glass. She laid down, curving her body toward the handheld camera. Grabbing it, she did her best to pull energy from the battery, trying to kill the camera as well as give herself a boost. She didn't have Snow's adeptness with electronics, but she was able to find the energy and pull a great deal of it into her.

She sheathed her knife for the moment and closed her eyes as she sat back up. Mental image, she reminded herself. She felt the weight of what she wanted at her belt, and as she reached for it, she only hoped it would actually work. There was no way she was going to leave Liam alone and at the mercy of souls that had been so evil in life that they had received a death sentence, even if it was to get help for him. There was also no way she could magically get him back to Aiden and Teeny, at least not that she knew about.

The feel of the radio in her hand was achingly familiar and her hand wrapped around it, pressing the button as if it hadn't been months since she had used one. "Andy," she said and released the button, holding her breath.

Andy Halleran sat in his car, keeping watch on the approach to the prison, making sure no one came into the area to interfere with the TV show filming. He had heard some weird noises coming from the prison but hadn't really paid it much mind. Everyone knew the stories about the place, and sounds were a usual occurrence here.

He jumped when his radio flared to life, the static loud in the quiet car. He picked up the radio and faintly heard his name being spoken by a familiar female voice. He blinked, looking at the receiver, feeling a little numb. He knew Cadence was a ghost, and with Aiden here, he thought there was a chance she could be here as well, but he hadn't expected this.

He picked up the radio and pressed the button. "Cade?"

Relief flooded Cadence as she heard his voice, sounding far away and tinny on her radio. She had no idea how much she would be able to get through the radio before the extra energy she had stolen from the camera would give out. "Andy, trouble. Help. Gallows." She could feel the drain on her strength with each word she spoke, so she knew she had to be short. Silence filled the room as she waited to see if there would be a reply.

It felt like an eternity, but she knew it was only a few seconds before she heard his voice, full of static and sounding very far away as he said, "10-4."

CHAPTER 25

Prison Fight

Snow couldn't believe that the young woman was still trying to communicate with him, even though he had made it abundantly clear that he was not willing to talk. He was still captive in the box, his head bowed, unmoving and unresponsive to the continued nattering of Teeny. He did have to admit that she had just as strong a stubborn streak in her as Cadence did.

Aiden sighed and ran a hand through his shaggy brown hair. "Teeny, if this is the real deal, why isn't he responding?"

"What do you mean by that?" Teeny was indignant that Aiden could suggest the person in the box was a fake.

"Well," Aiden said, lowering his voice, "you guys did say you had tricks up your sleeves if things were boring here." He shrugged, leaving the suggestion at that. It almost physically hurt to accuse the young woman of trying to fake evidence, especially when he knew how real what they had was, but he had to try anything to discredit what they were seeing.

"Seriously?" Teeny rose to her feet, advancing on Aiden, which was somewhat comical given their height difference. "Jesus, Aiden, I thought you, of all people, would be happy with this. This box works; we trapped a spirit."

"Yes, a spirit that doesn't look like it belongs here, and who isn't talking," Aiden countered. His conscience hurt at the fact that he was trying to throw shade on something that had worked and that he knew she had to have spent hours on. He had no other choice, however. There was no way he was going to be able to convince them to bury the footage, so all he could do was try to frame it as a setup.

"I thought we had already agreed that he must have been a detective that got caught here during one of the riots and killed." Teeny wasn't about to let the challenge to the validity of her work go.

"I mean, it's possible, yeah," Aiden said with a sigh. He wondered why Cadence hadn't come up with a way to free Snow. "Maybe there's something wrong with the audio components of the box? Maybe we should take a look?"

"We heard him talk. Granted, only one word, but still," Teeny said, arguing that nothing was wrong with her box trap.

"True. I'm sorry for saying something might be hinky about it," Aiden relented. "I'm just frustrated that we can't get anything out of him. Maybe we should let him go and try to get one that's a little more responsive."

The tension in Teeny's shoulders seemed to ease a bit as Aiden backed off of the assertion that the box was a fake or some kind of trick. "Maybe," she said. She checked her watch and frowned. "Where the hell is Liam?"

"Maybe he is having better luck out there than we are in here," Aiden said with a chuckle.

"I hope so. I hope Liam doesn't run into something like I did back in solitary," Teeny said.

"You want to go check on him? I haven't heard any of those demon train sounds coming from that way in a while," Aiden said.

"Nah, it's fine. If Liam is having luck, he will kill me for interrupting him. But if we haven't heard from him in another half an hour, I'm going to buzz him on the radio. Luck be damned," she said.

Snow was glad that, at the very least, they couldn't hear what he was hearing. Even over the buzzing of the electrical field he was caught in, he could hear the screams and howls coming from the gallows and whatever inhabited that area. To Snow, it seemed that the cries were growing louder.

A loud thudding from the entrance grabbed the attention of the ghost and two breathers alike. Squeaking hinges echoed loudly in the building, followed by thudding footsteps that were running right toward them. Teeny rose to her feet as she and Aiden shone their flashlights in the direction the sounds were coming from, watching a light bounce its way toward them.

Andy ran into the room and stopped, taking only a moment to process the setup in front of him before looking over at Aiden. "The gallows? Have you been there yet?"

"No, but Liam is out there," Aiden answered.

"Why?" Teeny asked, moving closer to the detective. Concern was clear on her face.

"Where is it?" Andy asked, looking tat Teeny. "Point the direction."

"I'll do better than that, this way," Teeny said. She took off running, knowing that the detective would have absolutely no issue keeping up with her short stride.

As their footsteps receded, Aiden looked at the box and at Snow. He ran a hand through his hair and turned, walking behind the camera he had been doing his best to block earlier. He then stopped the recording and quickly did the same for the camera strapped to his chest. "No more recording for now," he said. He then took a step toward the box but stopped, his eyes going wide.

Roy Pruitt stood in front of Aiden, his arm outstretched, his hand disappearing just under Aiden's coat. Aiden couldn't see the ghost, but he could feel the burning of the touch on and in his chest. He also saw Snow stir in the box.

"Let him go," Snow said, having heard Aiden's promise of no cameras recording.

"Now, why on earth should I do a thing like that?" Roy asked. "Way I figure it, you and that filly of yers didn't really come here 'cause of the two in the gallows. You came tied to this guy an' his friends. I didn't miss yer girl touching this one, tryin' to talk to him."

"Not ... tied..." Aiden tried to gasp out the words. He couldn't really hear the conversation, but because Roy was touching him, he was getting the gist of it. He was also aware that the spirit impaling him was full of anger, hate, and bitterness at pretty much everyone. And that he was desperately trying to protect a secret here.

"This prison is our jurisdiction; we would have been here regardless if this young man was or not. Because we have jobs to do, Mr. Pruitt. You have a job to do, as well, if you haven't forgotten. One that includes protecting breathers from the spirits in your charge." Snow wished he could be making these arguments on his feet instead of cooped up in a box. He was aware that his authority was taking a bit of a beating by being captive.

Roy turned his head to one side and spat. "Job," he said, and the bitterness in his voice was evident. "The dead shouldn't have jobs. We put in our time on that hamster wheel. Should be sun, sand, women, and beer from now on. And that's what we're gonna get."

"What do you mean by that?" Snow just wanted to distract Roy and get him to let go of Aiden.

"Doesn't matter," Cadence said, materializing beside Roy and not hesitating. She moved like lightning, her fist, and every ounce of power she could muster, connecting with Roy's cheek. The force of the blow sent Roy reeling, and he lost his grip on Aiden. Roy glared at Cadence and disappeared, teleporting off to somewhere else in the prison.

Aiden gasped and staggered back a few steps as he was released, though his chest still burned where Roy had touched him. He was shaky, feeling a little weak and lightheaded. Aiden didn't know if Snow had managed to get the guy to let him go or if something else had happened; he was just glad to be released. He got his equilibrium and hurried to the control panel of the box. He flipped a couple of switches, and the box turned off, releasing Snow.

"Stay back," Snow said to Cadence, who had stepped forward to help him. "Just in case," he added with a bit of a smile as he got to his feet. He was glad to be free of the damned thing and owed Aiden a debt for doing all he did.

Aiden saw Snow disappear and looked around. "Sorry that took so long, man," he said to no one in particular.

Andy overtook Teeny as they ran for the gallows building in the prison yard. He threw open the door and held it for Teeny. He undid the holster latch out of habit and looked at Teeny.

"You stay behind me until I say it's clear. Got it?"

Teeny nodded, feeling her heart pounding in her chest. Fear for Liam had overtaken her, as she hadn't been able to raise him on the radio as they had run.

Andy opened the door to the viewing room and left Teeny there to hold it open as he went down the small corridor. "Shit," he said. "Clear, get over here."

Teeny wasted no time running after Detective Halleran, and her eyes widened as she saw the destruction in the room. The seats, which had been bolted to the floor, stood in the same place they always had. But the room was littered with broken glass.

Andy had already crossed where the glass had once been installed, his footsteps crunching the broken shards on the way. The light of his flashlight illuminated the fallen form of Liam on the concrete floor beneath the gallows, as well as the small pool of blood coloring the glass beneath his leg.

"Liam!" Teeny yelled and ran over to where he was.

"Careful of the glass," Andy said, and while he was aware his voice was sharper than he meant for it to be, he also knew that if he didn't warn her and make sure she heard him, he might have two injured people to get out of here.

"Oh my God, his leg." Teeny breathed, seeing the grotesque shape it was in. She used her flashlight and looked up, seeing the open floor above them.

"His weight must have made the hinges on the floor give out or something," Andy said. He took out his cell phone and called 911. As it rang, he looked around for signs of Cadence, not knowing that she had teleported out as soon as he had gotten to Liam's side. "Look, I'm calling an ambulance. I need you to go tell Aiden to direct them here, okay?"

"I can do better than that," Teeny replied, pulling her hand radio out of her pocket. "I'm not leaving Liam."

Whatever was going on in the gallows room, Aiden knew it had to be a sticky situation. Andy Halleran would not have just come barreling in on his own for no reason, asking about that specific room. However, he had no idea if it was something serious or if it was some kind of distraction Cadence had created to pull Teeny away from the box so he could get Snow out.

What Aiden did know was that there was real danger here. He could feel it in the atmosphere, piling up. The way his flashlight didn't seem to send the shadows away as much as it had earlier in the evening. The oppression he felt bearing down on his shoulders. The anger and hatred he had felt when whoever that Pruitt ghost was had touched him. That spot still hurt on his chest.

Cadence and Snow knew there was a danger, too. The only difference was they could see it. The few ghosts that remained in the prison, the intelligent ones, at any rate, were gathering around them in the rotunda. Bits and pieces of darkness were slipping in as well, coming from the direction of the gallows room. Whatever Roy had done had set them free.

"Weren't there more of them earlier?" Cadence looked at the handful of ghosts, and she was sure there had been more in the cafeteria when they had been in there with the investigators.

"Yes," Snow said with a nod.

"And still no sign of Pruitt," Cadence said, her voice quiet.

"Yes, well, I've a feeling we haven't seen the last of him. He might just need a little time to get over being punched that hard by a woman." Snow did nothing to hide the smile of pleasure from the memory of Cadence walloping Pruitt in the face.

Cadence grinned a little as well. "Yeah, well, at least this time, I got to facilitate your rescue for once, instead of the other way around."

"Don't worry, darlin'." Roy's drawl came from behind a couple of the prisoner spirits. He still had a silvery smear of blood on his face from his nose and lip where Cadence had punched him. "I'm sure yer gonna need rescuin' in just a little bit here."

Aiden was busying himself with packing up some of the equipment when his radio screeched to life, startling him.

"Aiden, it's Teeny, you copy? Over."

He pulled the radio from his pocket. "Yeah, Teeny, I copy. What's going on?"

Teeny's voice crackled a little as it came through the speaker of the radio, and Aiden could hear the emotion behind her words, even though he had no idea what was going on. "We have an ambulance inbound; send them back to the gallows building. Over."

"Ambulance? You guys need me to help?"

"No, stay there," said Teeny. "Just send them back here. I'll catch you up soon. Out."

Aiden looked at the now silent radio in his hand and pocketed it with a sigh. Something had apparently gone very wrong with Liam. He only hoped it wasn't something too bad.

"Where are all your charges, Mr. Pruitt?" Snow leveled his icy gaze at the mustachioed guard. "Given the way you've behaved tonight, I can't imagine they are all in their cells, behaving nicely."

"These are my charges," Roy said with a shrug.

"No, we checked the counts a couple of days ago to prepare for this particular place," Cadence said. "Not counting residual, there should be roughly thirty active spirits here, including you. I see nine."

"Did you kill them, Mr. Pruitt?" Snow asked the question as Roy began to walk around them.

"Gonna definitely kill you two, so what does it matter what happened to them?" Roy sneered and made a lunging move toward Cadence but backed off as she pulled her knife.

"It matters, and if you're going to kill us, what's the harm in telling us?" Cadence said with a shrug.

"Let's just say they been set free an' leave it at that," Roy said, giving a nod to his group of prisoners. "Kill the old man first. The girl is mine."

The eight prisoner spirits that were left ran for Snow, who teleported to the other side of the box, standing between it and the hallway out to the yard and gallows room. The bits and pieces of dark souls that had been set free from the gallows room were swirling around the hallways and rotunda area.

Cadence teleported to Aiden and touched his arm. He stiffened, but then relaxed as he recognized the touch. Her other hand held her knife, and she didn't take her eyes off of Roy as he began to come after her. She quickly teleported away, materializing near Snow, who almost took a swing at her, thinking she was one of the prisoners.

"Sorry," he said, then turned his attention and fist to the next nearest one.

Cadence didn't bother with fisticuffs. She'd had her fill with this place and the spirits in it. As one of the prisoners ran at her, she let him impale himself on the knife. His eyes widened with almost comical shock at what had just happened.

"Might want to get the fuck back in your cell, inmate," she said with a growl.

The prisoner didn't argue; he just did as she said. This caused a couple of the other prisoners to pause. Snow had already beaten two others into submission, and they were unconscious on the floor. The two inmates who had paused teleported back to their cells as well.

The three left standing in the rotunda beside Roy reacted a little differently. One tried to grab one of the unconscious ones, but Snow stepped over the prone man and shook his head at the prisoner. The man backed off, throwing his hands up in the air. As Snow bent down to put the prone prisoner in handcuffs, another one thought he had an opening and materialized a lead pipe into his hand. He ran and jumped, aiming to bring the pipe down on Snow's head.

The pipe made contact, but not with the back of Snow's head. It hit Cadence's knife. Both Cadence and the inmate felt the reverberations of that impact up their arms. She looked the man square in the eyes and said, "Boo." He teleported away, as did the other prisoner, who had managed to get the second unconscious inmate away as well.

Snow stood over the now handcuffed unconscious prisoner, Cadence standing beside him as they both looked at Roy. "I honestly would suggest that you simply allow us to take you into custody, at this point, Mr. Pruitt," Snow said.

"That ain't gonna happen," Roy said.

"Drop this one off," Cadence said, nudging the handcuffed one with her foot as she spoke to Snow. "I can handle him."

"Cadence," Snow said, shaking his head.

"No. I have this. Trust me," she said firmly.

Roy chortled. "Whoo, boy, wouldya look at that. The filly thinks she can handle me, huh?"

Snow frowned. He didn't like the idea of leaving Cadence alone, especially since this was her first case back after being so severely injured. But he knew the look in her eyes. He knew she had a plan. He also knew she felt the need to prove herself after what had happened with Overton. So, he nodded to her and disappeared with the prisoner.

Cadence looked over at Roy as he spoke. "Girly, you got no idea what you just let yourself in for."

She smiled as sirens could be heard approaching. She was still on the other side of the box from Roy, and Aiden was still packing the gear up, working on the camera that had been near the box, oblivious to the spiritual goings-on around him. She held up two fingers, the back of them facing Roy as she channeled her favorite character from the old Mortal Kombat movie.

"Let's dance," she said.

Roy teleported right in front of her, but she was prepared for that. She lashed out with her knife, and he danced away, but not before she got a good slice in across his forearm.

"You'll " he began, but she cut him off.

"What? I'll pay for that? You assholes really need to find better material," she quipped. "Try answering a few questions for a change. What are you up to here? Where do you keep buzzing off to?"

He growled and came at her again, this time not trying to grab her, but with fists flying. She teleported to the other side of the box, close to where Aiden was working on taking down the tripod for the camera. He let out a roar of frustration that even Aiden heard, as he paused in his work, looking around.

"You'll tire out before I do," Roy said, his voice a growl. "I know yer hurt. An' I know you've been puttin' out a lot of energy tonight. Then it won't matter what's goin' on in the rec room. You'll just be a smear of silver blood on the floor."

"Then what are you waiting for? I'm right here, tired and injured," she taunted. It wasn't a lie. She was definitely feeling the drain on her energy, and the stinging in her feet was becoming more persistent. "But thanks for the heads up about the rec room," she added with a sweet smile.

He teleported behind her, which was a move she hadn't expected. He pushed her down onto the floor from behind, and she rolled to one side, her leg passing through Aiden's leg. Roy moved to pounce on her, and as he landed, she mustered everything she had and threw him at the box while yelling, "AIDEN!"

Aiden knew his cue and dove for the box, flipping the control switches and bringing the box back to electrically humming life. Roy became visible inside the box, imprisoned. Aiden blinked in surprise and took a step back as the prison guard roared once more in frustration and anger. Roy began trying to beat his way through the force field walls of the box, only to meet with the same resistance and pain that Snow had gotten when he had tried.

"Aww," Cadence said, feigning sadness and pity. "Beaten by a girl. An injured and tired girl at that. Must be a big blow to that huge macho ego of yours."

"You goddamn whore," Roy bellowed. "You have no idea how much trouble you are in right now."

"None, I would say," Snow said, materializing beside his partner. He walked to the box and passed into the field.

"Snow, what are you doing?" Cadence asked.

Aiden made his way toward the entrance of the prison, letting Cade and Snow deal with the other ghosts on their own. The sirens had become loud, and he could see red lights bouncing off the walls in the lobby.

"I'm taking him in," Snow said, his voice calm as he clamped handcuffs on Roy. "Be so kind as to short out the box so I can leave it before the medics get in here."

Cadence nodded, knowing time was short. She took a moment and took aim with her knife, throwing it into the control box. Sparks flew out of the box, and the field went down. As it did, Snow disappeared with Roy.

"Straight back, through the doors," Aiden's voice said, echoing down the hallway from the rotunda. Hurried footsteps echoed as well, and Cadence watched as the EMS team hustled with the gurney.

Aiden followed behind a little slower, but paused in the rotunda, noticing that the box was dark once more. "Cadence, if you still do that dream thing, I would like to put in a request for one because I would love to know what the hell was really going on here tonight." He then hurried to catch up to the EMS team.

Snow materialized once more beside Cadence. "That was a damned good job, Riley," he said.

"Thanks," she smiled. "Pruitt did let something slip."

"Oh?"

"Yeah," Cade said. "And it makes sense. What is the one room that none of us bothered going into because of its reputation?"

"The rec room," Snow answered. "Is that where he has been disappearing to?"

"From what he said, that's what I would guess," she said.

"Shall we check it out?" Snow didn't wait for a reply. He knew Cadence far too well. He knew she wouldn't leave this place without looking into it.

"Absolutely," Cade said, following Snow.

"What's gone on while I've been tied up?" Snow gestured toward the hallway that led out to the gallows.

A noise drew their attention that way before Cadence could answer. The EMS team was hurrying as fast as they could with their rolling gurney, which was now occupied by an unconscious Liam. Teeny and Aiden followed; Teeny didn't even notice that her experimental box was turned off.

"I'll meet you at the hospital. Thanks, Aiden," she said, tossing him the keys. Aiden stopped in the rotunda, and Andy stopped beside him as they both watched the woman and EMS team head out.

"You have any idea what happened back there?" Andy asked.

"No, I was here with Teeny. Liam went off on his own," Aiden said. "How did you know to come in and where to go? Riley?"

Andy nodded as he watched the lights of the ambulance begin to recede as they drove away. He then turned to Aiden. "Yeah. I don't know how, but she managed to get me on the radio and let me know there was trouble and someone needed help in there." He sighed and rubbed the back of his neck, his brain still working on figuring out the ghost stuff. "Come on. Let's lock this place back up. Their producer can come get their equipment in the morning."

"Sounds good to me. I can't wait to get out of here," Aiden said.

"Neither can I," Andy said.

"Neither can I," Cadence said, echoing the two breathers left in the prison. "But we have one more stop to make first."

Snow and Cadence crossed the distance to the rec room, passing through the barricade and the door without a problem. Cade was moving slower than usual, and Snow was worried about her. He was also quite aware that he had not fully regained feeling in his arm from trying to punch his way out of the force field. He had a feeling they would both be paying a visit to Ramon later.

They stopped in unison as they entered the rec room. Rusted pipes hung down from the ceiling, plenty of room to hang people from, like in the history Derrick had given the day before. Cobwebs and dust covered every corner and any piece of furniture left. Most of the furniture was in place against the door, a further obstruction to those trying to enter the room. This left most of the floor clear. The floor itself had been destroyed. The dirt underneath the flooring remained and had a circle dug into it.

The circle was large enough for a couple of people to fit in comfortably. Snow and Cadence walked closer, trying to find anything special about it. There were no candles, no other symbols, no special stones. It was just a circle in the dirt.

"I wouldn't get too close."

The voice came from behind them, and both Cadence and Snow whirled around, Cadence with her arm already cocked back, ready to punch. The man between them and the door was wearing an inmate's uniform. He had short black hair and was clean-shaven. He threw up his hands in a defensive gesture.

"I don't mean harm, I swear," he said. Cadence recognized him as one of the inmates who had backed off when she had stabbed the other one.

"You didn't seem to not mean harm earlier," Cade said, putting her arm back down.

"I had orders." He shrugged. "They don't mean anything now that Pruitt is gone."

"What's your name?" It was Snow who asked the question.

"Roland," the inmate answered.

"Who gave you orders?" Cade watched Roland, wary of the man as she spoke.

"Pruitt. Now that he's gone, I can't get out, so that's not worth defending anymore," Roland said with a gesture to the circle.

"Portals," Snow said, his voice a soft murmur. "And they're not taking me with them."

Cadence looked over at Snow, an eyebrow lifted in curiosity. "What?"

"The madman in the solitary cell that attacked the young lady," Snow said. "He knew inmates were getting out through some kind of portal and was getting upset that he was getting left behind."

"Digger?" Roland laughed and shook his head. "Yeah, even Roy, rotten as he'd become, wouldn't let Digger out of this place."

Snow shook his head and looked back over at Roland. "How was Pruitt transporting people? There is nothing special about this circle."

"It's less to do with this circle and more to do with what's on the other side of the portal when it's opened. I have no idea how Pruitt did what he did, but he was getting us out. The rumor was we were getting to take over bodies and live again," Roland said.

"Why tell us this?" Cadence was suspicious of the man and his motives after everything that had transpired.

"I was in for armed robbery," Roland said. "I had two weeks left on my sentence. Two weeks. Then the riot that killed Roy happened. I got caught in the crossfire, so to speak. I was going to get out and start trying to put my life and family back together if I could. I didn't want to follow the same path that brought me here. Not everyone who died here stayed as bad as when they walked in."

"So, you're just trying to help us out from the goodness of your own heart?" Cadence couldn't keep the skepticism from her voice or face.

"Yes, Ma'am. Ain't like I can go anywhere now, anyway. I wanted to go through that portal to whatever was on the other side, have a chance to live again, on the right side of the law this time." Roland shrugged. "That was the only reason I followed Roy's orders. I knew he'd gone south, but the hope of getting away, and maybe this time getting it right, blinded me to just how far south he had gone."

"Was Roy working with anyone that you know of, Roland?" Snow's stance relaxed as it became evident that this Roland was no threat.

"Yeah. Not sure who, but there was someone on the other side of the portal. I kind of always got the feeling that whoever it was over there was the one making it work, not Roy," Roland said.

"Thank you, Roland. I appreciate your forthrightness," Snow said.

"And I appreciate you going back to your cell instead of making me fight you," Cadence added with a bit of a smile.

Roland returned the smile and nodded. "Hitting women, alive or dead, was never how I operated." He then disappeared.

CHAPTER 26

Catching Up

The waiting room at the hospital was crowded, full of people waiting to be seen and waiting to be let back to see those they brought. Lauren and Derrick sat amidst the sick and impatient while Doug and Robin were in the back with their daughter as her foot was tended to.

"Didn't expect to see you two here," Aiden said, walking up to them as he and Andy walked into the waiting room.

"Aiden!" Lauren couldn't conceal her surprise. "What happened?"

"Liam got hurt pretty badly. Teeny is back there with him now," Aiden said. "EMS brought them in."

"You might want to get that chest seen to," Andy suggested to Aiden. Andy then turned and wandered toward the triage area and spoke quietly with a nurse before he was buzzed back into the emergency department proper.

"Your chest?" Derrick asked with concern.

"I got attacked. It's no big deal. Could've been much worse," Aiden said, trying to shrug off their worries. "Why are you two here, though? What happened with the family?"

Lauren looked around and then urged Derrick and Aiden to follow her away from the main waiting area, down a hall. "Emma kidnapped Ava from the house. Sam was able to follow and let me know where they were. Ava is okay for the most part, except that she stepped on a nail, so they have to remove that, and she'll probably need a tetanus shot."

"Poor kid," Aiden said. "What the hell is the ghost kid up to, anyway?"

"Sam is working on getting her to leave the family alone," Lauren said. "It's strange, though. There was someone else at the house tonight, a person. Whoever it was cut the power to the house. That's when Emma took Ava. Sam was able to get the other little girl to move on. I just hope he can convince Emma to leave the family alone."

"Think he'll convince her?" Derrick asked.

"I guess we'll find out," Lauren said with a sigh. She then lifted her gaze to Aiden. "Your turn. What happened at the prison?"

"Well, I'm glad you weren't there. I'm not sure you could have handled it. Teeny was practically attacked by the spirit of some madman whispering horrible things in her ear while we were investigating solitary confinement and death row. The cafeteria was lively too. I somehow got locked into a death row cell for a bit. And Teeny had an experiment she was running. I have no idea if that experiment is what led to what happened, but this is going to be one hell of a situation to explain."

"What do you mean?" Derrick asked.

"She had this experimental box that she built, the size of a big dog cage," Aiden said. "Whatever it was, it worked. Snow got trapped in it." He kept his voice low, aware of the fact that their conversation could carry if they were too loud.

"Holy shit," Derrick said, his eyes wide.

"Yeah," Aiden said with a nod. "This isn't going to be easy because he was visible and audible. Then we started hearing these weird noises from the gallows building out in the yard. Liam went to investigate. Teeny didn't want to leave her experiment, and she didn't want to be alone after the whole solitary incident."

"So, Liam went to the gallows on his own?" Lauren asked, unable to fathom an experienced ghost hunter making such a decision when the reputation of where they were investigating was so evil.

"Yep," Aiden confirmed. "I'm not sure what happened, but he got hurt pretty badly." Aiden paused, looking around to make sure that they weren't being listened to. "Detective Halleran was already there. He was the off-duty officer that they hired to work as area security for the night. I'm not sure how she did it, but Cadence managed to call Andy in to help. He came running into the prison and knew he had to get to where the gallows were."

"When did you get attacked?" Lauren asked.

"Right after Andy and Teeny took off for the gallows room. I stopped the cameras and was going to turn off the box to let Snow out, but something caught me. It was like some hand had reached into me and had a hold of my bones."

"Show me," Lauren said. Aiden lifted an eyebrow at her, but she shook her head, her "den mother" role in full effect. "Show me," she ordered.

Aiden sighed in resignation and began to unbutton his shirt beneath his open coat. He hadn't even looked yet, and he was hoping there would be nothing to see. He was wrong.

"Oh my God," Lauren said, her voice just a breath as she took in the damage. A hand shape was visible on Aiden's chest beneath his brown chest hair. The color varied, going between an angry red and a vivid purple. "You should probably get seen, too, Aiden. To make sure there isn't any worse damage."

"I'm fine, Lauren. It's just a bruise. Stings still, but I'm fine," Aiden said.

"Aiden..." she began, but then she backed off with a sigh. "Fine, but if they say you should be checked out, will you do it?"

"They?" Aiden asked, not sure to whom she was referring.

"Our friends," Lauren replied, trying to keep it vague.

"Fine, if they think it is more serious, then I will get it checked out. But we've all been scratched or bruised before. It's never been anything more."

"Except for Dan," Lauren said.

"Lauren, that was a whole different situation, and you know it," Aiden said, putting a comforting hand on her upper arm.

"I know. I just … I don't want the same thing happening to you because we ignored something serious," Lauren said.

"Don't worry," Aiden said, offering his friend a smile. "I'm not going anywhere."

"Where are they anyway?" Derrick asked.

"Not sure," Aiden said with a sigh, leaning against the wall. "Cadence and Snow had to deal with taking someone into custody, whatever that means for them. I have no idea if they came back or are still dealing with that or with the prison."

"Wait, they took someone into ghost custody from a prison?" Derrick asked, not sure if he found the idea unbelievable or just hysterical.

"Yeah, I know how it sounds. There was a whole thing that was going on with them. Not sure if the prisoners were trying to riot again or what, but I think that the guy I helped them trap in the box was the monitor for the prison."

"Like Sam was for the dorm house?" Lauren asked.

"Yeah," Aiden said.

"What do you mean, you helped them trap him?" Derrick asked.

"At one point, Cade touched me. I don't hear her like you do," he said to Lauren, "but I got images, intentions from her. She needed me to turn the box back on when I heard her yell. I waited, heard her yell, turned the box on and there was this other guy. Snow stepped back in and cuffed him, took him away."

"Anyone else finding this ironic and absurd?" Derrick was shaking his head, trying to wrap his brain around all of this. "The monitor for a prison, a bad guy that the ghosts we know had to remove from the human prison and take to ghost prison?"

Aiden smiled. "We're in a strange position, Derrick. We know more than most people do about what goes on over on the other side of the veil. Just because we know it, however, doesn't mean it is always going to make sense to us."

"Amen," Lauren said.

Cadence and Snow entered the hospital waiting room behind Andy and Aiden. They noticed Derrick and Lauren at the same time as the two other men did, and Cadence looked over at Snow.

"That means Sam is here," she said to him. Snow nodded, and they turned, leaving the breathers to catch up, to go in search of the younger Riley sibling. They passed the nurses' station and rooms for treatment. They finally saw Sam in a room that had a little girl asleep on the bed, wrapped in blankets. She had a parent on each side of her holding her hands as a nurse was working on bandaging her foot.

"Sam," Cadence said, beckoning her brother out to them.

He looked a little surprised to see them here and went out into the hallway to join them.

"What brings you two here?" Sam asked.

"One of the television guys got hurt pretty badly," Cade said. "He's around here somewhere and is probably going to be here for a few days. I can't imagine he is not going to need surgery. And what the hell happened to you?" Her eyes had not missed the thin silvery thread around his neck, which mirrored the wound of his near decapitation.

"I'm not hurt," Sam said, deflecting the question.

"What happened with the little girl?" Snow asked.

"Turns out that Wolf guy was pulling the strings on the whole thing. He summoned Emma, not knowing that he would get Sarah in the deal as well. He wanted Emma to escalate the haunting to get our ghost-hunting group drawn in to investigate. He somehow knew that they had ties to someone involved in the Irene Woods case you guys did a couple of months ago."

"So, he was deliberately trying to get our ghost hunters involved in a case that would take place during the time of the television investigation?" Cadence looked at Snow, trying to make sense of it. "Why?"

Snow frowned as he thought. "The obvious answer would be to try to get our guys to ignore the television group and go with the case involving the family and the little girl. But you are right to ask why, Cadence. Leaving the television investigators unattended and unassisted by our breathers? Or does he know more than he should? Did he know that would split us up, and some would have to attend the prison and others attend the family?"

"That's a reach, though, isn't it?" Sam looked at Snow as he asked the question. "I mean, the breathers don't know what we do."

"Don't they?" Snow looked back at Sam as he replied. "Our group knows quite well what goes on, much as I dislike that break in the rules. If this man summoned the spirits of the girls, as you say, he might well have a great deal of knowledge. Let's not forget that this Wolf person also had the recipe for the non-human chaos being that killed Dan Kurtz and that we barely managed to get rid of."

"And he was somehow involved in everything that went on with the dorm house, too," Cadence added. "Remember, he is who Overton called for help when they had Andy in the basement of your dorm."

"I guess it isn't that much of a reach then," Sam admitted with a shrug. "But if that's true, then what the hell is going on? Why did he need to split us up?" He was still holding on to the fact that he had recognized the face of Wolf. His sister had already had one hell of a night.

"I have a guess as to why," Snow said, weighing his words. "Assuming that Wolf knows about how we work on this side of life, he could have wanted to split us up to hide what was going on at the prison."

"What do you mean?" Sam's emerald eyes looked between Snow and his sister, and it was his sister who answered.

"Something was going on there. Most of the active spirits were gone. There were maybe ten to twelve that we saw in the cafeteria, but then by the end of the night, there were only nine, and that included that asshole Roy."

"How were they leaving?" Sam asked.

"There was a portal circle in the rec room of the prison," Snow said. "After the fracas, another prisoner explained that the portal led to somewhere else, that Mr. Pruitt had been sending inmates through the portal with the promise of freedom and a flesh-and-blood body to possess, to live again. However, the person on the other side of the portal, the one who seemed to be the person making it work, that is what we don't know," Snow said. "And that is what bothers me."

Wolf tossed his coat on his couch. He was tired and getting far too old for this crap. That Ava girl would have been a great student; she had such skill at seeing and communicating with the spirits. But now he was afraid that he had lost her. He was going to have to be careful with any plans regarding her in the future, at the very least.

He went to his kitchen, pulling a bottle of water from the fridge. He paused, looking at a picture on the wall. It was a picture of the day he got his promotion to police captain. "How did I let this get so damned far?" The question was to no one, as he was alone in his apartment.

"Oh, please. Are you lamenting your position?" A familiar voice came from the hallway that led from his living room back to his bedroom. A shadowy figure stood there as if he had been waiting for Wolf all night.

"No, I'm not," Wolf replied, straightening up and setting the bottle of cold water on the breakfast bar that separated his kitchen from his living room. "I simply dislike scaring children."

"I told you when you were a teenager that you were going to need to check your conscience at the door," the figure replied. "Some things we have to do may not be pleasant, but they are necessary. It is for the greater good that we do this."

"I know," Wolf sighed. "I'm aware. If your plan can be brought to fruition, it will help us all. I'm on your side, Shaldoxz, you know that. My devotion to the cause has never wavered. Not once. Not when I have to put aside files the coroner sends me. Not when I have to lie to my officers about what really happened at a crime scene. Not even when I have to bury one of my best detectives."

"Captain Rodriguez," Shaldoxz said. "The death of your best detective had nothing to do with our plans, and you know that. In fact, all it's done is complicate them. I know what you have had to do has been hurting you. Trust me when I say it will all be worth it in the end. Immortality is one hell of a reward."

"Is it working? Have the tests you have been running been going smoothly?"

"Well, that's the problem we had tonight. Even though you tried to split them up, they were still far more successful than I had anticipated. The group was even short one of their usual team members. Your cult is going to have to work on finding another place with spirits that want out. But up until tonight, things were going well."

"Is there another student candidate other than the girl from tonight? I doubt I'll be able to get anywhere near her again, thanks to the brat you had me summon," Captain Rodriguez, aka Wolf, said.

"Give it a few months and try again," Shaldoxz said. "By then, I'll have moved Snow and Riley onto some other contrived emergency, and they'll have forgotten about the girl. But mark my words, Wolf. Do not screw up again. My patience with mistakes is fading quickly as time grows closer."

"How are you able to direct Riley and her partner?" Wolf asked, taking a swig from his water bottle.

Shaldoxz stepped forward into the light, and his usual form melted into one Wolf hadn't seen before. His wavy ginger hair was wildly unkempt, and he was shorter than usual, with a little weight to him. He wore slacks, a button-down shirt, and a sweater vest, with glasses covering his eyes. Whitfield gave Wolf a smile.

"Because they trust me," he said.

Book Club Questions

1. How has Cadence developed as a character?
2. Do you think Snow was right for being worried about turning into a monster?
3. What are your thoughts on Croft?
4. Prior to the end of the book, what were your thoughts on Whitfield's absence?
5. How do you feel about the development of Ramon and Cadence's relationship?
6. What do you think about Sam's character and his development?
7. Who did you think Wolf would turn out to be? Were you right?
8. What are your thoughts on what Pruitt was hiding in the rec room?
9. Do you think we have seen the last of Emma?

10. With the last sentence of the book, do you think that reveal was the truth? Or something masquerading as him?

Author Bio

Growing up in a haunted house and having a father who loved horror set the stage for Amanda's creative life. This Urban Fantasy author has been writing since her teen years, blending horror, fantasy, and the paranormal. Amanda balances a day job, her writing, her family, and helps her husband run a board game group and YouTube channel, *Tabletop Misfits*. Local to Southwest Florida and a total geek, you can often find her at conventions, either as a vendor or an attendee.

Cadence and Snow will return in Dead Revelations

Paul paused and opened his attaché case, pulling out a plain manila file from it. "This is the info I have on the house. It isn't much, but it should be enough to spur on super research man here," Paul said with a thumb gesture to Derrick, who was sitting to his left. "It's sad to admit, but I've always been hesitant to do the research myself. I am a bit afraid of what I might find, since my family is connected to the place."

"That's understandable," Lauren said. "Have you ever been to the property before?"

"No," Paul said with a shake of his head. "I guess I'm more superstitious than either my dad or uncle were. I don't want to invite trouble if it is there to invite."

"That's a smart decision, to be honest," Aiden said, as Derrick pulled the file over to him. "You have no idea how many people decide to go looking for stories and legends only to find out that they are true in the worst ways."

"And most of them aren't prepared to deal with it," Derrick added as he opened the file.

"We'll take the case, but we won't be able to get out there for a couple of nights. Last night was a little rough, and I'd like to give Derrick time to work his magic," Lauren said. "Do you want to be with us when we investigate the property?"

"Is it necessary?" Paul's apprehensiveness showed as he asked the question.

"No," Lauren said with a calming smile. "But we will need the keys to the house if you aren't going to be there."

"Sure," Paul said, pulling his key ring out of his pocket. He detached a second key ring from it that had a simple blue plastic tag on it, as opposed to the Harley Quinn comic book character on his main key ring. "The key to the house is the big one. The smaller key is for the padlock on the shed. At least that's what I've been told."

Lauren took the keys with a smile and a nod. "Derrick has a way to contact you, right? We'll let you know before we plan to go in, and then a day or two later, we'll let you know what we come up with. Sound good?"

"Sounds good," Paul said, reaching over to shake the hands of the three of them in turn. "I appreciate it." The professor gathered his things and headed out, Derrick walking him to the door to lock it behind him. The college senior then returned to the table his friends were at.

"So, what do you think?" Derrick asked.

"I think you forgot to order extra sauce on the meat in my pho," Aiden said as he ate.

"He seems genuine," Lauren said, giving Derrick a straight answer. "I like the fact that he is cautious. Can you tell anything from what he gave you?"

Derrick sat back down and began looking through the papers in the file. After a moment, he let out a low whistle. "Guys … This place is Scarecrow Farms."

Aiden nearly choked on his pho.

More books from
4 Horsemen Publications

Crime, Detective, and Noir

A.K. Ramirez
Secrets & Photographs

Joe Davison
Journey to Hell

Mark Atley
Too Late to Say Goodbye
Trouble Weighs a Ton

Paranormal & Urban Fantasy

Amanda Fasciano
Waking Up Dead
Dead Vessel

Beau Lake
The Beast Beside Me
The Beast Within Me
Taming the Beast: Novella
The Beast After Me
Charming the Beast
The Beast Like Me
An Eye for Emeralds
Swimming in Sapphires
Pining for Pearls

Chelsea Burton Dunn
By Moonlight

J.M. Paquette
Call Me Forth
Invite Me In
Keep Me Close

Jessica Salina
Not My Time

Kait Disney-Leugers
Antique Magic

Lyra R. Saenz
Prelude
Falsetto in the Woods: Novella
Ragtime Swing
Sonata
Song of the Sea
The Devil's Trill
Bercuese
To Heal a Songbird
Ghost March
Nocturne

Megan Mackie
The Saint of Liars
The Devil's Day
The Finder of the Lucky Devil

PAIGE LAVOIE
I'm in Love with Mothman

ROBERT J. LEWIS
Shadow Guardian and the
Three Bears

VALERIE WILLIS
Cedric: The Demonic Knight
Romasanta: Father of Werewolves
The Oracle: Keeper of the
Gaea's Gate
Artemis: Eye of Gaea
King Incubus: A New Reign

FANTASY

D. LAMBERT
To Walk into the Sands
Rydan
Celebrant
Northlander
Esparan
King
Traitor
His Last Name

The Inbetween
Hannah's Heart

LOU KEMP
The Violins Played Before Junstan
Music Shall Untune the Sky

R.J. YOUNG
Challenges of Tawa

DANIELLE ORSINO
Locked Out of Heaven
Thine Eyes of Mercy
From the Ashes
Kingdom Come
Fire, Ice, Acid, & Heart
A Fae is Done

VALERIE WILLIS
Cedric: The Demonic Knight
Romasanta: Father of Werewolves
The Oracle: Keeper of the
Gaea's Gate
Artemis: Eye of Gaea
King Incubus: A New Reign

J.M. PAQUETTE
Klauden's Ring
Solyn's Body

KYLE SORRELL
Munderworld

DISCOVER MORE AT
4HorsemenPublications.com